Just Shut Up and Drive

by

Chynna Laird

Just Shut Up and Drive
by Chynna Laird
Published by Astraea Press
www.astraeapress.com

This is a work of fiction. Names, places, characters, and events
are fictitious in every regard. Any similarities to actual events
and persons, living or dead, are purely coincidental. Any
trademarks, service marks, product names, or named features
are assumed to be the property of their respective owners, and
are used only for reference. There is no implied endorsement if
any of these terms are used. Except for review purposes, the
reproduction of this book in whole or part, electronically or
mechanically, constitutes a copyright violation.

For my Gramps. Thank you for your unconditional love, guidance and kicks in the butt when I needed them most. You will always be with me.

Chapter One

"You want to do *what*?" eighteen-year-old Wil Carter asked his grandfather.

Gramps Wilf clicked his tongue. "I know you aren't deaf, my boy. I *said* you and me are going for a road trip for a week or so in the summer."

Wil shook his head, picturing being crammed in his puny hatchback with his ninety-five-year-old grandfather. For "a week or so." Sounded like the start of a really bad cheesy movie: "The Adventures of Young Dude and Grumpy Old Man." Wil thought of more than a fistful of things he'd rather do than drive hundreds of miles with a grouchy old geezer. But he knew there was no use in putting up a fight. He'd end up doing exactly what he always did: what he was told.

All Wil wanted to do over his summer holiday was work over at the corner drugstore and hang out with his buddies. After all, it was going be his last summer in Winnipeg before he headed out east to go to university. But, no, Gramps had set his plan in motion, yet again, without him even knowing.

"Gramps," Wil said, releasing a sharp breath. "You know that I work at the pharmacy every summer. How am I supposed to earn up my tuition if I'm chauffeuring you around the country? Besides, Mr. Bassey isn't going to give me that much time off. He's short-staffed and—"

"Already taken care of," Gramps interrupted, shuffling over to his favorite recliner, backing up to it, and then plopping himself down. "Jim said he could spare ya for the time we're gone by getting the other gals to take their holidays later. Done."

Wil allowed his jaw to fall slack. "Uh, Gramps? Did it ever dawn on you that, maybe, I'd like to... oh, I don't know... have some fun this summer, being that I have to go to university in the fall?"

Gramps flipped the footrest of his recliner up, scootched his body back, then folded his hands across his belly. He tilted his head down, staring into Wil's pale blue eyes over the rims of his Buddy Holly-styled frames. "What? You got a girlfriend?"

"Well, no."

"Big plans aside from workin'?"

Wil put his hands on his hips then looked up at the ceiling. "No."

"Doin' anything special on your days off aside from slackin' off with those freaky friends of yours at the beach, starin' at those girls you only wish could be your girlfriends?"

Wil looked back down at his grandfather. "Ouch, Gramps. And, yeah. Hello? I said I wanted to have some fun."

Gramps grabbed the remote from the armrest. "Mmm-hmm. Well, 'fun' should be spent doin' things you're interested in and good at."

"Well I'm interested in sitting on the beach, and I'm good at looking at girls. C'mon, Gramps. It's summer. And it's the last one I have in high school. Some of my friends are moving away to go to school and—"

The old man leaned forward and pointed the remote at Wil, who took that as a cue to shut it. "Let's get something straight, son. You're still living under my roof. I know you're a man now and want to be makin' all your own choices, but there's still plenty of things you need to learn about life before you'll make it on your own. And I'm gonna teach you those things this summer. I got some important things I need to show ya. I said we're goin' on a road trip, and that's exactly what we're doing. Now either sit on down and watch the news with me or find something more useful to do."

With that, Gramps pressed the remote with his thumb and Wil heard the TV blaring behind him. The two men glared at each other for a few seconds, then Wil dramatically flopped himself into the green-and-white-checkered barrel chair beside his grandfather's recliner. He put his elbow on the armrest then leaned his cheek onto his fist.

"Can you at least tell me where we'll be going?"

"No."

"What? Why not? If you're going to kidnap me, I should at least know where I'm going. Especially since I have to be the chauffeur."

"We're just gonna make a few stops between here and the other side of Saskatchewan. You'll find out soon enough. And by the way, if I'm kidnapping ya, then you don't need to know exactly where you're goin', now do ya? Since you're the driver, you just gotta go where I say."

From the corner of his eye, Wil saw his grandfather's mouth tug up into a little smirk. Then Gramps cranked the volume loud enough for any passerby outside to hear the news right along with them. Another subtle sign that their conversation was done, at least from Gramps' perspective.

Wil squinted at the TV, heat radiating from the nape of his neck. *Great*, he thought. *A week or more of my summer vacation wasted with His Royal Crankiness*.

He wondered what his grandfather could possibly have left to teach him. Or if he really wanted to know.

****

Later that night, Wil lay sprawled out on his bed waiting for sleep to come. The dry heat of the house suffocated him, so he shoved his covers to the bottom of the mattress. Gramps kept the heat on all year long due to his ever-increasingly bad circulation, not that he'd acknowledge it. And since Wil's room was on the second floor, all the heat seemed to rise up and get trapped in his room. He pretty much sweated out the summer months.

He folded his hands behind his head, hoping for a cool breeze to come through his wide-open window. Gramps would have had a moose if he'd known he paid for heat that was just flowing out the window. *But, seriously. Put a sweater or blanket on, old man!*

Wil breathed in deeply, allowing the air to slowly escape through his nose. *Oh well.* At least there was some relief from the 1890s-style steel fan blowing across his body from his desk. He closed his eyes.

The fan made a metal clank every few seconds. The occasional car zoomed down the avenue behind the house. The old pipes whistled and popped. Every so often, Gramps' snores rumbled from the main floor.

He shouldn't have been such a jerk to his grandfather earlier. Experience taught Wil the harder he tried resisting his Gramps' orders, the more stubborn the old fart got in making sure they were carried out. Then, suddenly, a dude finds himself foolishly traveling across the Trans-Canada Highway for part of his precious summer vacation. And since the entire "vacation" would be between Winnipeg and the Alberta-Saskatchewan border, the view would be nothing more than: flat, flat, flat... oh, a cow... flat, flat, flat... oh, a bale of hay. Then being stuck in his small car with Gramps barking orders at him like a drill sergeant with hemorrhoids was enough to drive the most even-tempered guy batty.

4

Especially when considering the fact that Gramps wasn't a decrepit old man, but a feisty old dude full of fire and thunder. The man had more energy than guys Wil's age. And with his attitude being he's old enough to do and say whatever he feels like, he got himself into more trouble than a toddler in a china shop. But Gramps said he had some things Wil needed to see, and when Gramps Wilf gave an order, you flipping well stepped in line or got a "whopping." Or at least a verbal one.

Wil rolled over on his side and sighed. He opened his eyes, barely making out the picture on his nightstand. He reached out for the old wooden frame, hovering his fingers over the foggy figures, then grabbed it and pulled it closer to his face.

Wil had been only five when his parents died. He barely remembered them. He recalled coming home from kindergarten the day his parents were supposed to have been back from their vacation, and his Aunt Jaquie being there instead of them.

"You have to come back with me to Gramps' house, Wil," she had said. "I packed a bag for you. Go get whatever else you need for bedtime."

He had pouted. "But I was over there for a long time. Today was when they were supposed to come back. They promised they'd be here."

There'd been no real explanation for what had happened. Aunt Jaquie had just said something about a terrible accident and that Wil had to stay with Gramps until things were... sorted out. That had been thirteen years ago.

Wil's mom had been an only child, but his dad, Gramps' son, had been the oldest of five kids. He had other aunts and uncles that he could have stayed with, but he'd heard they'd all decided Gramps was the best person to raise him. Guess they had been afraid he'd have turned down a wrong path from having had a "bad start." They had figured he needed someone who'd be firmer with him — to keep him on the straight and narrow. He guessed it had been the best decision under the circumstances.

Gramps was the only parent Wil had ever known. He guessed the old man loved him, or he'd never have taken him in. But Gramps sure never made things easy on him. And there had never been an overwhelming show of emotion or loving tenderness between the two of them. Wil figured it had to do with him being a boy, and Gramps wanting to make sure his grandson grew up strong, not needing anybody else to depend on.

Just like him.

As Wil had gotten older, his parents' faces seemed to fade… just like looking at their picture in the dim light. And it hurt. He still heard his mother singing his favorite lullaby. He felt the sting of a baseball in the new leather glove his dad had bought him when they'd practiced catch in Gramps' front yard. But their faces felt a little less vivid with each passing year.

Maybe the trip would do Wil some good. Gramps might want to teach him a few things, but maybe he could learn more about his parents too.

And himself.

He replaced the picture on the nightstand and rolled over on his stomach, drying his cheeks on his pillowcase. He'd play the smart-butt to his buddies about the dreaded trip. "Yeah, gotta take the old man on a stupid week-long field trip. Blah, blah, blah."

Secretly, he'd use the time as a way to find answers of his own.

The fan blew cool air up across his back, fluffing his hair around like his mom used to do for a second then traveled back down his legs. After a few more flips and flops, he was lulled into a restless sleep.

Chapter Two

Wil had the worst sleep. So he wasn't impressed with being shaken awake just as daylight blared through his window.

"Blast it all, boy! Get up!"

"Gramps, for the love of all that's good in the world. It's Saturday. I don't have to work, and I just want to sleep in. With all due respect, and there isn't much at the moment, get out!"

"You pick your lazy butt up off that bed and haul it downstairs in the next five minutes, or I'll pour all the coffee down the sink."

Wil opened his eyes as wide as he could. He made out the fuzzy image of his grandfather perched on the edge of his bed, the man's hand still on Wil's forearm. "What is your problem? What can't wait for another couple of hours?"

Gramps didn't answer. He just stood up, gave Wil one last shake then walked out.

Wil rolled over on his back and put his pillow over his face. *I wonder how much time I'd have to serve, offing a guy his age,* he thought. *Really. The courts would be empathetic if they knew what it was really like to deal with him.*

He groaned, threw his pillow across the room, and then lugged himself up to a sitting position. He reached down and pulled the same clothes on that he'd worn the day before. If Gramps made him get up that early, Wil wasn't going to make an effort to look and smell all pretty.

As he walked down the stairs, the sweet aroma of coffee flooded his nostrils. Gramps was nowhere to be found, so he took the time to pour himself a cup of coffee then yelled, "Gramps?"

No answer.

"Gramps? Where are you? You wake me up before the sun has made a full appearance, and you are nowhere? Gramps?"

Still no answer.

Wil stirred cream and sugar into his coffee, turning the caffeine-packed liquid from black to a caramel color. He side-glanced to the back hall and noticed the inside back door was wide open. He tapped the spoon on the rim of his cup, tossed the spoon into the sink, then sucked a big slurp of coffee.

Ahh. A few more gulps and I'll feel half-human.

He walked over to the back hall, cup in hand, and stuffed his feet into his runners. He figured Gramps must have been out in the backyard, watering the garden or tinkering in the garage. Since he had no explanation of what he was supposed to check out, Wil figured he was expected to search it out. Not uncommon.

"Gramps? C'mon, you old goat. This hide-and-seek thing is getting lame." Wil raised his cup to take another sip when Gramps' voice startled him, causing him to drool hot coffee down his front.

"What are you doing out here? I told you to meet me in the garage."

Wil cursed under his breath then rubbed the coffee drips on his T-shirt. "Um, actually you didn't. You just ordered me downstairs."

"Hmph. Guess I hoped you'd be smart enough to come out here since I left the door open."

"I think you just had your hearing aid turned off."

"What are you rambling on about?"

Wil took a deep breath in through his nose then released it slowly before replying. "Nothing. My mistake, as always. I'm coming. Just excuse me for a second or two while I nurse the third-degree burns on my chest."

"Not my fault you have a problem with drinking."

"I don't have a drinking problem."

"You're right. The problem is getting it anywhere near your mouth in the first place, obviously."

"All right! That's enough, already!" Wil raised his free hand. "It's too early for this, and I don't have enough coffee in me to deal with you. Just tell me what in blazes we're doing out here and what specifically I'm supposed to be doing."

Gramps walked up in Wil's face, gripping his wrist. "Let's get something straight, son. You don't talk to me that way. That sort of disrespect is exactly why we're going on our trip. Like I told you yesterday, you got things to learn… things to know… before you can be a real man in the world. Just like your dad did. He learned. You're gonna. Now get your sorry butt in that garage before I kick it across the street."

Wil yanked his arm free from Gramps' deceptively strong hand and stormed into the garage. Hot tears stung his eyes, which he hated. He wasn't a crier and he certainly was never sensitive to his grandfather's spout-offs. Must have been the mention of his dad.

The garage was smaller than most of the other garages in their neighborhood. But it was big enough to fit Wil's run-down hatchback and some other vehicle that had been covered up by a blue tarp since Wil had moved in. He was never allowed to touch it or even know what was under it. The one time he'd tried peeking, Gramps went off on him so badly he was afraid to ever go near it again. It just became some sort of mysterious relic like all of the other things in the garage. And down in the basement. And up in the attic.

Beside the vehicles were three wooden shelves packed with mason jars filled with different kinds of screws, nails, bolts, and other things Wil neither recognized nor cared about. Under that was a small, double-door tool bench. A car jack, a crowbar, a few dirty rags, and a few other tools were scattered across the top of the bench.

Wil frowned then put his coffee down. "What's going on, Gramps? What is all of this stuff?"

When he turned around, his grandfather stood in front of the tarp. "When your daddy found out he was having a boy, he went out and found a special gift for ya. Guess he figured it could be something the two of you could work on together. Here. Gimme a hand with this thing, will ya?"

Gramps bent down, grabbed the bottom of the tarp with both hands then pulled. Wil rushed over to help. His heart pounded. He wasn't sure whether it was from excitement, curiosity, or the joy of being given a part of his father.

The two men slowly pulled the tarp back, gently tugging back around each crevice and part. When the vehicle was finally revealed, Wil stared at it with his mouth hanging open, the tarp still clutched in his fists.

It was a classic pickup truck with the most beautiful fire-engine red paint job he'd ever seen. "Gramps. Is that a 1955 F100?"

"Yep. Your dad got it for a steal from one of his buddies' fathers. He was just gonna send it to the dump to get crushed. Your dad took it off his hands, then he and a few friends worked on it the whole time your mom was pregnant."

Wil walked around the truck, running his hands over the body. "It has a school bus chassis, body, and grille. The tires are more modern, and I have no idea how they got this backseat here, but it's... awesome!"

"Yeah, that took the longest. Guess he figured with another person coming along, he needed another seat."

"Why didn't you ever tell me about this? Or show it to me? You know how much I'm into cars."

"Your dad didn't want you to see it until you were old enough to help him work on it. Then, well, he passed on, and I just had it moved in here. Kept it polished, did things here and there, you know. Until I thought you were ready."

Wil's throat tightened. "You mean… this is mine?"

"It's your dad's. But I think his plan was for you to have it once it was all fixed up. You took those automotive courses in school. I'm thinking you can help take over the maintenance for me on this thing. Besides, I ain't traveling with you in that unreliable, crappy thing you drive around in."

The young man spun around to face his grandfather. "You mean, we're going to drive this on that trip you want to take? For *real?*"

Gramps nodded. "Here's the deal, son. You help me get that old truck up to snuff in the next two weeks, and we'll drive it. You got time with exams and classes being over. Do it around your shifts at the drug store, now. No ditching anything else for that truck, or I'll cover it back up. Deal?"

"You got yourself a deal, old man."

They both took on the same stance — legs apart, one arm hugged across the chests, the other holding their mugs — and stared at the old truck, sipping their coffee.

For the first time in as long as he could remember, Wil actually felt good about his situation. He was happy living with Gramps, but never felt like he really… belonged there. They cared about each other, yet had always kept each other at an arm's length. Maybe it had been because his dad, the part that was supposed to connect the two of them, was missing.

That day, they finally had a way to bond. And for the first time in way too long, he felt his dad with him too.

****

There wasn't as much to do on the truck as Gramps had made it sound. But it did need a tune-up. A rather old-fashioned term considering most modern cars just needed to be taken to a local car dealership to have things repaired or replaced. Wil loved that he was finally getting to use some of the skills he'd learned in his automotive courses.

Wil had hated school and had gotten into trouble for skipping. In fact, he'd missed so many classes at one point, there had been concern he wouldn't graduate. Wil knew he had put Gramps at his wits' end trying to get him motivated. So the old man had arranged for Wil to take the car class for extra credit, as well as an incentive to stay in class and hit the books.

His automotive teacher, Mr. Hendricks, had taken Wil under his wing, appreciating his love for cars. Mr. Hendricks was also the school counselor, so Wil kind of figured Gramps had had an ulterior motive for getting him into the class, which he had been really ticked off about at first. There was no way he was going for counseling, no matter what Gramps thought.

But after a few weeks, he had felt better about it all. Not only had he gotten to learn about and work on cars, but Mr. Hendricks had also turned out to be a pretty cool guy. He had let Wil go in during lunch breaks or after school when he wasn't working, to do extra work. And he had just *listened* to Wil.

He had never given him advice or any counselor mumbo-jumbo. All he'd ever given him was his knowledge and his time. That was something Wil had appreciated. He never admitted it to Gramps but the experience really did help Wil get through high school. And now he finally got to work on a real car that he was going to get to drive. He made a mental note to take a picture of his work and send it to Mr. Hendricks.

It was the Wednesday before the date Gramps had set to leave on their road trip, and Wil had the day off — his only day off that week before they left. So he planned to get as much of the harder, more time-consuming tasks done as he could, then just tweak until launch day.

He opened the hood of the truck then stared. It was in mint condition. His dad and his buddies had done an outstanding job. And Gramps must have kept it up a lot more than he let on because everything looked near perfect and new.

"What's the plan for today?" Gramps' voice came from the garage door behind Wil. He fingered wires and engine parts while Gramps' familiar shuffle scraped across the garage floor and stopped beside him.

Without looking up, he said, "I was thinking of replacing the plugs and testing out the points and condenser. If I have time after that, I'll adjust the carburetion, change out the timing belt, and maybe change the transmission fluid."

"Hmm. That's a lot for one afternoon. Maybe just focus on the ignition system for now. I'm bettin' you'll find other stuff to check out, touch up and look at as you get in there. Your dad always did."

Wil paused, keeping his eyes on the engine. "Gramps?"

"What?"

"Did you work on this with Dad too? You know… hang with him and stuff?"

"He wouldn't let me do anything on the truck — it was *his* project. But, sure, I hung out with him. I handed him tools, we talked all about cars and all the shoptalk. You know, I do know a thing or two about vehicles."

Wil sputtered a laugh. "So I've heard." He gave Gramps a quick side-glance then put all his focus back under the hood. "Well, uh. Maybe you could hang out here with me? You know… like you did with Dad…"

"Sure, son. That'd be fine." Wil got a whack on his upper

back, then Gramps left his hand there for a few moments.

"But if you touch anything, I'm going to have to slap your hands and send you inside."

"Any chance we could suck that sarcasm outta ya before we go on our trip? One of us won't make it otherwise."

"Only if we lose yours. And don't worry. I'll make sure you have the funeral of kings."

"Just shut up and get to work. You're wastin' daylight."

Wil smiled as he felt another hard pat between his shoulder blades, then the hand moved away.

For the rest of the afternoon, Wil worked on the truck while Gramps perched on a stool talking about old cars and engine parts, and occasionally handing Wil a tool. He'd never realized how cool it must have been to be alive long enough to see cars go from jalopies to fancy sports cars.

Close to suppertime, they decided to call it quits for the day and cover the truck back up with the tarp.

Wil rubbed engine oil off his hands and forearms with a rag then said, "Thanks for this, Gramps. Really. Just… thanks."

Gramps nodded. "Sure, son. But you're doing me a favor. Not only are you doing all the work, now I don't have to sit in that cramped, flaming-hot, junky hatchback of yours."

"And here I thought you were doing this out of the kindness of your heart."

"Bah. You should know me better than that by now." Gramps waved his hand at Wil then walked toward the garage door. "Lock up and come inside."

"Be right in. I need to have a shower anyway."

Wil tossed the rag on the workbench, turned the lights off, and started out the door. He paused before shutting it, staring at the truck's form under the tarp.

I don't know what you have planned, Gramps, he thought. *But I plan to get to know you better by the time this trip is over.*

He slammed the door shut and ran into the house before Gramps had a chance to squawk out the order to do so.

Chapter Three

For all that's good and pure in the world, Wil thought as he flopped his head back on the top of his car seat. *What does a man his age need to pack up that takes this long?*

He'd been sitting in the truck for nearly fifteen minutes waiting for Gramps to come back out. The old geezer had been squawking at him since dawn to get a move on. They'd actually been in their seats, seatbelts buckled. Then Gramps had to run back inside to get something. "Run" being the operative word since he wasn't exactly rushing.

Wil lifted his head up, glanced over at the sidewalk, then let his head plunk back on the head rest again. His stomach grumbled. They'd decided to pick up breakfast from the coffee drive-through on the way out of the city so they could get an early start. He'd been up for over an hour with still no coffee or food in his system. Patience wasn't his forte at the best of times, but an empty stomach and lack of caffeine were enough to push him over the edge at that point.

He checked the time on the dash clock.

7:14.

That's it, he thought, pushing against the steering wheel

with both hands. *I'm giving him exactly one more minute, then I start honking.*

Gramps hated being rushed. And he really hated disrespect of any kind. The last time Wil had honked the horn at him from the driveway, Gramps had nearly twisted his ear right off his skull.

He put his palm on the side of his head from the memory then jumped when the passenger door creaked open.

"Well, welcome back." Wil sat up and leaned over the steering wheel. "I was about to send in a search party."

Gramps waved his hand at Wil. *"Bah!"* he grunted then reached back to pull his seatbelt across his chest. "I told ya I had to get a few things I'd forgotten to pack up."

"Well, I hope you went pee-pee while you were in there because I am not stopping for a while, mister." Wil pulled his seatbelt on, repressing a smile.

"If I have an urge, I'll just grab me an adult diaper from my bag," Gramps said with a deadpan stare. "Now shut up and drive."

Wil burst out laughing. *Well, I know who I got my sense of humor from.* "Okay. Are you ready?"

Gramps slapped his thighs, rubbing them with his palms, then gave a thumbs-up.

"Let's start her up."

Wil gripped the key already in the ignition then paused. He was actually nervous. His hands shook, his heart raced. He turned the key and the truck's engine sputtered once then clicked into action. Wil and Gramps looked at each other and grinned.

They held their stare for a few seconds, then Wil backed out of the driveway and eased into the early morning rush hour traffic on Kenaston Boulevard. After a quick stop at the corner store up the block, and much debate about who was going to pay, they were out on the highway.

"Good grief, boy!" Gramps yelled. "You drive like an old

lady on a Sunday afternoon drive. Don't be afraid to push down on that gas pedal."

"Gramps," Wil sighed. "I'm going the speed limit. Anyway, what is the hurry?"

"The hurry is I hate being a passenger, especially yours," he said, emphasizing each word. "And watch your mouth, boy. You aren't too old for me to give a whoppin' to."

"You're just ticked because they won't let you drive anymore. It's your own fault for not taking care of your eyes. And for the record, I'm not exactly thrilled at the moment having you as a passenger."

"You better watch your attitude, or I'll take this truck back."

"Correct me if I'm wrong, but it was Dad's, right? And I think you told me he wanted you to give it to me. Guess that means it isn't yours to take."

Gramps got a sour look on his stern face, like he'd just sucked on a lime. "Don't you be talking to me like I'm some crazy old coot who's lost his mind. I remember what I said. Shoulda charged you for it, considering the lip I have to put up with every time I'm gonna be in here with you."

"And what makes you think I'm going to drive you around everywhere in this beautiful truck? I'll chauffeur you around in my car."

"That piece of crap? Hmph. Forget it."

Wil stared at the road ahead of them. "You could take a cab, you know. Or the bus." *Sam Hill help the poor drivers.*

"Nah," Gramps said, slugging back the rest of his coffee and shoving the empty cup in a plastic bag. "I get much more pleasure out of torturing you than I would a stranger."

I noticed. "Alrighty, then. So you got a plan for us, or are we just going to keep going until we run out of gas?"

Gramps crossed his arms over his chest and looked out his window. "First stop is gonna be Elie."

Wil released a sharp breath and squinted. "Seriously?

There's like 100 people living there."

"Six hundred and fifty."

"Close enough. And I'm sure the census people were able to gather them all in one place and count them at once. C'mon, Gramps. What could possibly be in that small town worth checking out? If we drive straight on, we can get to Portage la Prairie for lunch—"

"Just because a place isn't all lit up like Vegas doesn't mean it shouldn't be visited," Gramps interrupted. "Some places need to be seen because they're gold mines for memories. We're stopping at Elie."

Wil had a smart-butt retort clinging to the tip of his tongue, but he held it there after giving Gramps a side-glance. The old man rested his chin on his right fist and stared out his window.

"Fine. I guess we're stopping at Elie," Wil mumbled.

Like my vote even counted.

For the rest of the road time to the small town, neither man spoke. Gramps held his position glaring out his window while Wil rested his head on his left hand and drove with his right. Nothing entertaining around but the yellow lines whipping under the front of the truck and the sound of the engine rattling in protest from the speed they were going.

Wil switched the radio on. After a second, and without breaking his stare out of his window, Gramps turned it back off.

Wonderful. Someone had once told Wil never to go on long road trips with kids, animals, or old people. They all needed pee breaks every two hours, got restless sitting still for too long, and bit you when they were mad.

At least Elie was only a twenty-minute drive.

****

When Wil saw the sign for the turnoff to Elie, he almost

cheered out loud. Not out of enthusiasm to see the place, but more out of relief to get the stop over with. As he pulled onto the gravel road leading into the town, Gramps said, "Your driving style will be perfect here. Speed limit in town is only forty-five miles per hour."

Wil shook his head. "Well, things must get to just about at a standstill on Sunday afternoons then, hey?"

Gramps clicked his tongue, keeping his eyes straight ahead. They passed by a few pockets of houses and what looked like an old-fashioned general store. A couple of half-ton trucks were parked outside, two guys leaning out their windows talking. A small group of ladies gathered outside the store doors, laughing.

Wil wasn't about to say it loud enough for Gramps to hear, but he thought the small-town mentality was kind of cool. Everyone knew each other and took time to check in with one another. They seemed to genuinely care about their neighbors, not like in the city where people never took time to even acknowledge who was around them.

Guilt gnawed at Wil's gut. He knew one of them had to extend the olive branch, and it sure as heck wasn't going to be old Mr. Grumpy Pants. Wil drew in a deep breath then bit the bullet.

"Look, Gramps. About earlier… I'm sorry I was such a jerk. You're taking me on this… journey… and I should be more respectful. I mean, I'm still not thrilled with the whole shebang but, well, I promise to play nice. If you do."

Gramps sniffed then shrugged. "Yeah, all right. All's good." He elbowed Wil in the arm and said, "I'd be happy if you just acted your age. If you can do that, I can."

Wil let out a belly laugh. "Holy crap. I don't think the world is ready for that." He quickly sobered, remembering what he was trying to do. "So? We're good?"

"We're good. Okay. Go through downtown here right through to the end. I'll tell ya when to turn off after that."

"Downtown" Elie was one long, two-way strip with small stores on either side. There were a few clothing stores, a bakery, a coffee shop, a couple of stores selling knick-knacks, and a variety of other Mom-and-Pop type shops. There weren't any of the trendy stores found back in the city, but there was everything a town needed.

They puttered down the street, passing only one other car along the way. Just as the cars passed, Wil and the other driver exchanged the old farmer's wave. Really it was just a nod and a gesture that looked like tipping a hat at someone. He wasn't sure who'd started it or when. It was just something you did in those small counties.

The drive through downtown seemed to take longer than the distance between Winnipeg and Elie. A plastic bag tumbling down the sidewalk, wrapping itself around street lamps along its way, went faster than the truck. But he couldn't step on the gas. How embarrassing would it be to be ticketed for speeding above forty-five? His friends would never let him live that down.

Gramps punched Wil's arm, snapping him out of his thoughts. "For crying out loud, boy! Pull your head out. I told you to turn off and now we went too far!"

"Ow! Man." Wil grimaced and rubbed his triceps. "That flipping well hurt, old man. I know you haven't forgotten how to talk. There are gentler ways of getting a guy to pay attention."

"Well, now, I'm sorry. But I called your name five times and got no response. I'd have twisted your ear but I couldn't reach up that far with this dang belt on me. Looks like you're the one that needs the hearing aid."

"Maybe I should just use yours since you never use it."

"I use it. I just turn it off when I don't like what I'm hearing."

"That's what I meant."

"That's not what you said."

"Whatever." Wil blew out a sharp breath. He made a U-turn in the middle of the road and then started back the way they'd come. "I seriously don't know how you got Gran to stay with you for so long. Did you drug her up with happy pills every day or something?"

"She had a hearing aid too."

Wil flicked Gramps a glance and smiled. *What a smart butt.* "By the way, you got quite a powerful right for an old dude."

Gramps tightened his lips as if he was repressing a smile. "Yeah, well… don't you forget it or I'll get 'cha again." He stuck his hand up in Wil's face and then pointed out his window. "See that white building over there? Turn… off… there. Got it this time?"

"Not sure. Maybe you should talk a little slower and enunciate a bit more for me."

Before Gramps had a chance to respond, Wil turned off where he'd been told and pulled up in the parking area in front of the building. Gramps was already getting out of the truck before the engine was shut off. It wasn't until Wil got out and saw the small cross over the door of the building that he realized it was a church.

There were bunches of white, purple, yellow, and pink wildflowers growing in patches beside the parking lot and church. A path wound around to the back area that was closed off by a gray fence. Wil could barely see over it, so he guessed it must have been just under six feet tall. Stone slabs and nameplates pushed into the ground gave away what the area was for.

Gramps walked up the wooden steps leading to the front door. "If you stand there with your mouth wide open like that, you're gonna catch mosquitoes or something. C'mon. Got someone I need you to meet."

Wil wasn't comfortable in churches. The last time he'd stepped inside of one had been for his parents' funeral. He and

God weren't exactly on speaking terms — at least not from his side of things.

Gramps, his aunts, and his uncles all went to church every Sunday. When she'd still been alive, Gran had insisted that everyone attended church services. It wasn't just for the social interaction, which she had loved so much. It was also so each of them became proper people, learning to respect others and treat the world kindly. Gran had died just before Wil had been born, but the family honored her wishes by continuing to go to church. Everyone, that was, except for him.

Wil got all the reasons Gran gave for going, he really did. And he had the highest respect for his grandmother. But he didn't feel he needed church to become the man he needed to be. He was a good person. He was responsible. He got good grades in school. He didn't smoke or do drugs, and he stayed away from the crowd that snuck off to the farmer's fields to drink every weekend.

Gramps may have made fun of his friends, but Wil surrounded himself with honest, fun-loving guys. Gran would have loved them, he was sure. And he worked his butt off every summer to pay his own way through university. He didn't need God. There was no room in his life for a person or being that would take his parents away from him so violently and without purpose.

"God doesn't make things happen to people," his Aunt Jaquie had said one Sunday in an attempt to get Wil to join them. "People make choices, and the results of those choices are what make things happen."

"He could have stopped the accident," Wil had said, refusing to listen to her cheap sermon. "Isn't He supposed to protect bad things from happening to good people or some junk like that? What kind of God would kill innocent people?"

"God doesn't kill people, Wil. He reaches back when they reach out to Him. You know, your dad could have waited out the storm. He *chose* to keep driving—"

"So it's my dad's fault?"

"No. I'm just saying that he chose to keep driving that night because he really wanted to get back to you, and—"

"Oh. So it's *my* fault, then."

Aunt Jaquie had sighed, putting her hands on Wil's shoulders. "It's nobody's fault. God didn't kill your parents or make that accident happen. It was just that. An accident. I was just trying—"

"Stop trying. Just stop. Nothing you or anyone else says is going to make me believe I need church or God or anything else like that. I'm not going, and you can't make me. Period."

And that had been the last time anyone had tried getting him to go to church. He figured if he kept his nose clean in every other way, they'd overlook it. He knew they talked about his lack of religious guidance or whatever they called it. He didn't care.

Wil shook his head to clear his thoughts and stood with his hands stuffed in his jean pockets. He stared at Gramps on the steps, shifted his eyes up to the wooden cross, then back down at Gramps.

"Oh, come *on*, boy. It's not gonna burn your skin when you walk inside!" Gramps shouted with his hands on his hips. Then his voice softened. "Look, there's no service going on right now. I just gotta talk to the reverend to open the back gate up for us, then we can do what we gotta do and leave. All right?"

Wil rolled his eyes then shuffled up to the steps. He put his foot up on the first step and said, "If it does burn, though, there's holy water in there, right?"

Gramps shook his head. "Trust me, son. If I can go through the doors each week back home unscathed, you'll be just fine."

The door creaked on its old hinges as Gramps gently pushed it open. *Yeah, this doesn't give off the vibes of a really bad 'B' slasher movie,* Wil thought as they walked over the threshold. He half expected someone to jump down on them from the ceiling fan or to find a serial killer lighting up a candle in the front, asking for forgiveness. He shuddered the thoughts out of his head as he followed on Gramps' heels to the front of the church.

It was about half the size of the church back home. There had to be only fifteen rows of pews divided down the middle by the gray-carpeted aisle they were walking down. The pulpit at the front was small with a microphone sticking out of the top. There was an old organ on the left side of the pulpit and four long rows of folded chairs set up behind it, arranged in a semi-circle. Wil figured that was for a choir. A table over on the right was covered with a long, white, satin runner and filled with thick, white candles. There were only a few lit at that time.

"Gramps," Wil whispered as they crept closer to the front. "I thought we are Protestant."

"We are. Why?"

"Well, I'm guessing that you went here at some point and the candle lighting thing is Catholic, isn't it?"

"This isn't just a church, son. There's a cemetery out in the back. It makes some folks feel better about losing their loved one when they can light a candle in their memory. Some do it, some don't. I like to."

Wil frowned. "Who are you lighting a candle for?"

"Gran."

Before Wil had a chance to ask any more questions, a voice came from the door beside the organ. "Well, bless my soul. Is that you, Wilfred Carter?"

The man wiped dirt from his hands on a small, flowered hand towel. He had to be in his early sixties, with a slight build, but not scrawny, and was a good six inches over Wil. His deeply tanned skin hinted to a lot of outdoor work. His eyes looked like two dark chocolate drops, and the deep wrinkles around his eyes and mouth when he smiled must have meant he did it a lot. There was something about the guy that made Wil's stomach feel warm from the moment he spoke. Not an ill feeling, but more a feeling of comfort and calm he hadn't felt in a long time.

"Well, look at you, John," Gramps said, holding his hand out for a handshake. "Happy to see you chose to stay here to run the church. Your dad woulda been proud."

This guy is a reverend? Wil didn't think he looked much like a church preacher. How many reverends wore jeans and T-shirts? Or had tattoos on their forearms? And weren't they supposed to wear those collar thingies?

The reverend moved to Gramps, enveloping the old man's hand between his own. As if reading Wil's thoughts, he said, "Things are a little more casual these days. We don't need to wear our reverend garb unless we're on official business." He winked at Wil then said, "So, who is this young man, Wilfred?"

"Reverend John McInnis, this is my grandson, Wil. Wil, this is Reverend McInnis."

Reverend McInnis stuck his hand out to Wil. "Pleasure to finally meet you. My father, who was the reverend here for many years, baptized you. It was the one and only time you were out this way. Until today."

Still shaking hands, Wil looked over at Gramps. "I didn't know I was baptized," he said. "Or that I even had a connection to anyone out here."

"Well, you have a much deeper connection to this place than you know. But I'm sure your grandfather here wants to share all of that with you, knowing him."

The reverend let go of Wil's hand then said to Gramps, "I saw you pull up. The gate is already unlocked for you. Just lock it up behind you and leave the key in the mailbox out front. You know the drill, Wilfred. I'll leave you both in peace."

He pulled a jagged key out of his pocket and handed it to Gramps. "It's wonderful to see you again. Please don't be a stranger. And if you need me for anything... you know... don't hesitate to call me. Or get someone to call, right?"

"Thank you, reverend. I'll remember all that. Your father was a good man. He helped my family in many ways. That's part of why we're here."

The reverend nodded then swung his arm in the direction of the back door. "Well, she's waiting for you. Take care, both of you. I'll keep you both in my thoughts and prayers to keep you safe on the rest of your journey."

He gave Gramps a manly grip on the shoulder and then went to a room over behind the candle table that looked like an office.

She's waiting for you. What the heck did that mean? And who would be waiting for them out in a cemetery?

Wil wasn't sure he really wanted to know the answers to either of those questions.

But like it or not, he was about to find out.

Chapter Four

"C'mon, son," Gramps said, swatting Wil on the back as he walked past him on the way to the door. "Stop standing there lookin' so scornful or your face will stick that way."

Wil released a sharp breath. "Do you think, maybe, you could give me an order without having to beat me at the same time? That would be appreciated. By the time this journey ends, I'm going to be bruised head-to-toe."

"Well, if you didn't daydream so much I wouldn't have to keep shaking you awake."

"If you didn't talk so much, I wouldn't have a need to daydream," Wil said, closing the back door behind them.

Gramps grunted then opened the unlocked gate to the cemetery. "Grab a handful of those flowers there, will ya? Those are her favorites."

Wil was about to ask who "her" was again but decided to shut it. He knew he wasn't going to get an answer anyway. He just assumed whoever she was, she had to be a resident of the cemetery. Or his grandfather was finally losing it.

He bent over to pick the flowers, careful not to pull them up by the roots, and slid through the gate. The cemetery was about the same size as two decent-sized backyards found in the upper class areas back in Winnipeg. It didn't look like a 'rich man's' cemetery since a lot of the headstones were quite small. Most graves were marked with simple nameplates or wooden crosses. It seemed to be well taken care of, though, judging by the lush green grass growing around each guest.

There was a gorgeous willow tree in the farthest left corner of the fence, its branches hanging protectively over the nameplates around its base. There were other smaller trees spread out around the area, all with new leaf blossoms. One of the smallest trees standing beside a worn, faded wooden cross actually had a little bird's nest in it. Wil shuddered with the profound realization that past lives rested there while new life still sprouted all around.

I think Gramps is getting to me, he thought, shaking his head. He moved his eyes across the yard, stopping when he saw Gramps crouched down at a marker by the willow tree. He tiptoed over and around the path, silently apologizing to the names as he went, until he got to his grandfather.

"Here you go..." Wil started then stopped when he saw the name:

LILY-MAE CARTER (JOHANSSON)

Daughter, sister, wife, mother.

Rest In Eternal Peace

Gramps took the flowers and laid them in front of the small headstone. Then he said, "See, Mommy? I told ya I'd bring him one day. This here is Wil. Wil, this is your Gran."

Wil frowned, his mouth agape. "Gramps, I... why wouldn't you have told me this was what we're doing? It would have been nice to prepare myself."

"Don't you disrespect your Gran," Gramps said, his eyes still on the headstone. "I just introduced you to a fine lady. Now mind your manners, get down here, and say hello. She's waiting."

Wil had heard many stories of his grandmother's loving

nature, her wicked sense of humor, and her endless generosity. She was also one of the strongest women he'd heard of, having fought breast cancer not once but twice during a time when women weren't expected to live long after their diagnosis, no matter how hard they fought. She'd done all of that while raising five kids and taking care of the house while Gramps worked. She'd been the rock in their family and Gramps' entire world. To that day, he talked about her like she was still with them and always called her "Mommy."

Wil knelt down next to Gramps, giving him a quick glance. Then he cleared his throat and said, "Hi, Gran. It's nice to meet you."

The two men sat gazing at the headstone. A light breeze caught the branches of the willow tree, making one of the longer ones brush gently across Wil's cheek. Goosebumps exploded all over his body. He bit his lower lip in a lame attempt to stop tears from forming. He heard the tiny squeaks of the baby birds calling their mama from the nest a few feet behind them.

"We're just on a little road trip, Mommy," Gramps continued, his voice barely above a whisper. "Gotta teach this boy a thing or two. Just like I had to with Craig. You remember those days, right? Trust me, this boy is all sass just like his dad. But he's brains too so there's some hope." He coughed a weak laugh then said, "Well, we have to go for now. But you know I'll see ya soon. I promise."

With that, Gramps kissed the palm of his hand, pressed it to Gran's name, adjusted the flowers for her, then pulled himself up. He pushed his glasses up, wiped his eyes on the back of his hand, readjusted his frames, and shuffled down the path back to the gate. Wil stood, never taking his eyes off the headstone.

He'd never been to his parents' gravesite, and he didn't want to go. Somehow, the action of doing that would mean he accepted their death, and he didn't. He knew one day he'd need to, if for no other reason than to close the door on that chapter of his life. He wasn't ready for that yet, though. And no one pushed him on it.

But for some reason, visiting Gran was... okay. It was oddly comforting. It actually filled a tiny part of him that had been empty before he got there. It was hard for him to put into words, but the feeling was similar to the serene calmness that had enveloped him whenever his mom had hugged him after getting hurt or being scared. He smiled, shoved his hands deep in his front pockets, then followed Gramps.

They locked the gate and then went back into the church to return the key. Gramps started down the aisle toward the front doors of the church. Wil stopped and said, "Wait a sec. I have to do something before we go."

Gramps turned and waited as Wil lumbered over to the candle table. He lifted his eyes to the crucifix hanging on the wall above the candles. The smoke snaking up past Christ's face seemed to emphasize His anguished facial expression. Wil fought the urge to turn back around. He pulled his right hand out of his jeans pocket and picked up one of the long matches from the pile. He held it over the flame of the candle closest to him and, after a second, the end of the match sparked.

He moved his hand over to a thick, white candle that looked like it had never been lit, and touched the match to its wick. Once a small yellowish-orange glow grew, he pulled back the match and blew it out. He shoved his hand back into his pocket and stepped back from the table.

Take care, Gran, he thought. *Maybe I'll come back to visit again soon too.*

He walked backward toward the aisle between the pews where Gramps still waited, keeping his eyes on the crucifix. The smoke from the candle he'd lit weaved its way up to Christ's feet. A warm wave spread from the pit of his stomach out to the rest of his torso — not unlike the sensation of drinking hot soup on a cold day. Then he turned to face

Gramps.

The two men locked eyes. A smile tugged up the corner of Wil's mouth, and he nodded. Gramps nodded, and led the way out of the church. The old man put the key in the mailbox then walked down the stairs as Wil walked over to the truck and unlocked it.

They each got in, buckled up, and Wil started up the engine. They pulled out of the parking lot, drove back through downtown, and up to where the road met the highway. Then Wil leaned over the steering wheel. Both men stared out the windshield.

"Where to next?" Wil asked.

"Portage. We'll stop there for lunch."

"You're the boss."

As Wil turned onto the highway, Gramps leaned over and switched the radio on. He flipped through the stations until the sounds of early jazz filled the car, then he slumped back into his seat. After ten minutes of crooning, trumpet playing, and big band, Wil broke the silence.

"Gramps?"

"What?"

"Thanks."

Keeping his eyes forward, Gramps reached over and squeezed Wil's knee, patted it twice, then curled up against his window.

"We should be in Portage la Prairie in about an hour," Wil said, but from the soft snoring coming from Gramps' side of the car, he guessed the old man didn't hear him.

The yellow divider lines disappearing under the front of the truck were hypnotizing. The early afternoon sun shone right in Wil's face. He pulled the visor down then leaned back into his seat.

I wonder what Gramps has waiting for me at the next stop, he thought. He had a feeling that Gran's grave wasn't the only thing he was supposed to see on their trip. But he was ready for whatever was up Gramps' sleeve.

I hope.

****

"Gramps?" Wil said in a loud whisper, giving his grandfather a light shake. They'd arrived in Portage la Prairie, and Wil tried waking Gramps up from his deep slumber. The task was as easy as shooing a mama bear away from her cubs.

Oh, he'd so hate that comparison.

"Hey, Gramps. We're in Portage and I need help choosing where to eat," Wil said in a regular tone.

The old man clicked his tongue.

The old geezer probably turned his hearing aid off again. Well, I guess I'll have to pull out the big guns.

Wil turned on the engine then cranked the radio. When it didn't work right away, he turned it to a classical station just as a lead soprano hit her high note. Well, that did it. Gramps jolted awake, pushed himself up to a sitting position, and gripped his door handle. Breathing in and out for several seconds, he put his other hand on his chest. Wil leaned against his window, his hands over his stomach, in hysterical laughter.

Gramps glared at him and shut the radio off. "Holy Hannah, boy. If you were trying to kill me, that almost did the job. Don't wake a man in his nineties to the sound of a cat being shot with an elephant gun. This old heart can't take it."

"Oh, come on," Wil said, wiping his eyes and releasing one last snort. "Don't give me that. Your heart is as strong as any dude my age. Besides, that'll teach you not to turn your hearing aid off."

"Don't be so sure about that. You give the heart enough jolts like that and the end will come faster than you know. And stop harassing me about my ear hardware. If I wanna shut 'er off to get some sleep, I'm gonna."

Wil sighed and shook his head. "Fine."

Gramps looked around. "Where in tar nation are we?"

"Gas station."

"Good to see that we get two miles to the gallon. What a complete waste of money."

"You want me to drop you off at the bus station over there? I have no problem sending you on the rest of the way by yourself."

Gramps stuck out his lower lip and crossed his arms over his chest.

"Aw, turn that frown upside down, Mister Grumpy Pants," Wil said, flipping Gramps' lip with his finger. "Here. You can choose where we eat."

The old man swatted at Wil's hand. "Stop treatin' me like a child or some useless imbecile."

"Then suck that lip back in and act your age. Isn't that what you told me to do a few miles back?"

"Perry's."

"What's that, now?"

"I want to eat at Perry's. I got me a hankering for one of their Loaded Breakfast meals."

Just what Wil wanted right then. To watch an old man wolf down a plate piled high with pancakes, runny eggs, ham, sausage, and bacon. "Your doctor will kill me if I let you eat all that cholesterol, fat, and carbs."

"And how's he gonna find out unless you tell him? Look, a man lives over ninety he should be allowed to eat whatever the Sam Haiti he wants."

"I'll give ya that one. But I'm the poor sucker who has to be in a small space with you for hours after you eat all of that stuff, not Sam Haiti."

"Trust me, son. At this age, all food has the same effect on the gut. But I'd rather feel the effects after enjoying a Loaded Breakfast than gagging down a stupid bran muffin. And if you think I'm gonna eat a muffin and water while you're stuffing a burger and fries in your trap, you're nuts."

The two of the stared at each other for a few seconds, then Wil broke the silence. "Fine. Loaded Breakfast it is. But if you drop dead after eating it, I'm telling everyone you snuck off and ate it on your own. I'm not taking responsibility for it."

"I'd expect nothing less."

Wil drove across the main road to Perry's. The parking lot was almost full, but there didn't seem to be a long wait. They got out of the truck and started walking up to the door. Wil opened the door for his grandfather and said, "And for the record, I'm not having a burger this time. I think I'll go with chili."

Gramps pursed his lips. "Hmm. Too bad we don't have power windows in that old truck."

Wil let out a belly laugh and slapped Gramps on the back as he walked past. There were two families and one couple ahead of them.

"Should be about ten minutes or so at the most," the chipper hostess said. "Have a seat and we'll call you shortly. Did you have a booth or table preference?"

"Either is fine," Wil said, standing next to his grandfather, who'd taken the last waiting spot on the couch. "Just make sure to save us a booster seat."

"Oh. Do you have children joining you? We have crayons and activity books too."

"No kids. Just him. I'm sure he'd love the activity book, though. He gets a little cranky and impatient waiting for his food."

The people around them giggled. Gramps' face crimsoned. "Shut it boy, or I'll cut you out of the will. I already owe you for the opera wake up. Don't make me add another strike."

A little girl with dark hair and hazel eyes sitting next to Gramps tugged on his sleeve. He leaned down to her and she said, "Hey mister. Don't feel embarrassed that you use a booster seat. I do too. It just gets you closer to the food is all."

Gramps' lips stretched into a smile. "Why thank you, young lady. That's wonderful advice."

The hostess called the next name on her list. "Harper, party of three."

"Get up, Dakota," the woman said, yanking on the girl's arm. "Our table is ready."

"Hey. Take it easy there," Gramps said. "She's just enlightening us with her pearls of wisdom. She's a lot brighter than my grandson here."

The woman glared at Gramps, ignoring his comment and then disappeared down the aisle after the hostess. The slimy man with her, who looked like a lynch man from one of those mobster television shows, clicked his tongue at the old man, then sauntered behind the women.

Gramps looked up at his grandson, who shrugged.

Some people, man.

A few minutes later, they were ushered to a table in the back of the restaurant close to the kitchen. Since they both knew what they wanted, they were able to place their order right away. Gramps got a bottomless pot of coffee and Wil got an iced tea, also bottomless, although he never had more than one glass.

Wil sipped his tea then leaned back in his seat. He noticed the little girl and her… parents… sitting at the end booth a few tables away from them. Dakota sat on one side of the table coloring in an activity book while the couple sat together on the other side. They weren't even talking to her, completely engaged in their conversation. The whole scene felt so wrong and tugged on Wil's heartstrings. Why did some people have kids when they obviously had no interest in being parents?

His attention snapped back to Gramps, who was pouring another cup of coffee. "Hey. Take it easy on the coffee," he said. "Just because they call it 'bottomless' doesn't mean you have to take them up on it."

"Stop nagging me," Gramps said, stirring two creamers and two packets of sugar into his cup. "Excuse me for indulging in a few cups of good coffee. Stuff here is better than anything you've tortured us with back home."

"Nice. I only started making it because my gut couldn't take the army-style crap you were making."

"At least mine got ya goin'. With yours, I may as well have been just drinking decaf."

"Fine, whatever. Just don't suck back too much because we aren't stopping every five minutes for bathroom breaks."

Gramps looked Wil in the eyes and slurped up his coffee like they were eating in a noodle shop. The eyes of fellow diners around them burned into his skin from all angles. Heat rose into his cheeks.

"Very mature," Wil said. "If you keep this up, we won't need to stop in Selkirk for a coffee break. I swear, I—"

He stopped as commotion from the little girl's table made him turn around.

"Dakota, you stupid kid!" Mr. Lynch Man yelled. "You spilled pop all over my new jacket. You better hope this comes out or you're buyin' me a new one."

He flicked the back of Dakota's head with his knuckles then stormed off to the bathroom. Two waitresses and the hostess sopped up the spill while the woman with the little girl lectured her.

"Oh Dakota, honey. This is why we don't take you out to nice places. You're so clumsy and thoughtless. You've embarrassed us yet again. And you've upset Uncle Frank so much, he probably won't even want to stay."

Okay, uncle and aunt, Wil thought. But still. All that fuss over a spilled drink? Even Gramps didn't make a big deal about things like that.

"I didn't do it on purpose," Dakota said, her lower lip trembling. "It was an accident."

"Well your 'accident' got all over your uncle's jacket. Now we're going to have to go shopping instead of eat. That makes me grouchy."

That's it. "Gramps, I'll be right back."

"Be careful, son."

Wil swung his legs around and walked over to the booth. One of the waitresses finished wiping the table down with a cloth then put out new utensils.

"Excuse me?" he said. "I'd like to get the little girl another drink and have it charged to our bill."

The plump aunt sputtered a laugh and rolled her eyes. "Excuse *me* but that's really not necessary."

Wil kept his eyes on the waitress while he spoke to Dakota's aunt. "Well, I'm not getting it for you, so what you think is necessary doesn't matter."

She gasped. Suddenly Frank, who'd made a reappearance from the bathroom, was up in Wil's face. "Well it matters to *me*. The kid don't need another drink, see? She's just gonna spill it again anyway."

"Accidents happen, right, Uncle Frank?" Wil said, sticking his chest out and moving in closer to Frank. "Besides, it's just a glass of pop. What's the harm in it?"

Frank made a fist then seemed to clue in that most of the other patrons around them watched. He cleared his throat and ran his fingers through his overly-gelled, jet-black hair. "Yeah, right. No harm in it. Thanks. Now get lost."

Wil made his way back to their table. He lifted his iced tea to his lips to put the moisture back into his mouth, his hands shaking.

Gramps applauded, as did a few other people around them. Wil's cheeks prickled with embarrassment from the attention. "That was one of the best danged things I've seen, son. Good for you. I'm proud of ya, even if you do look like you're about to crap your pants."

"I was fine up until I saw him about to deck me." Wil's

hands finally steadied. "I hope we don't go out and find some grunt guys wanting to bust up our kneecaps or something."

The waitress brought their meals to the table. As she put Wil's chili and garlic bread down in front of him, she said, "That was a pretty cool thing you did over there. They come in here all the time and, well, that's the first time anyone has ever said anything."

Wil nodded. "Just make sure she gets the bottomless glass of pop, right?" He winked.

"Already taken care of. And no charge for the food. It's on us." The waitress smiled and went back to the kitchen.

Gramps sprinkled pepper on his eggs. "Gotta say, I'm starting to like hanging out with you."

"Sure, sure. Wait five minutes and you'll be barking a different tune. So? Does free food taste better?"

"I'd say so."

They ate their lunch in silence then sat back nursing the rest of their drinks. Wil looked over at Dakota's table and noticed she wasn't there. He turned his head around the room.

"She went to the bathroom a few minutes ago," Gramps said, slurping the rest of his fourth cup of coffee. "I saw her walk by while you were finishing up."

"I hope she'll be okay." Wil shoved his empty glass over.

"You can only do so much, son."

They got up and made their way back to the truck. When Wil opened his door, a cold slosh flooded his stomach. "Oh man. I forgot to lock it up before we went in."

Gramps stretched up to shout over the back. "I wouldn't worry about it. Mostly townsfolk and truckers stopping here, and there isn't anything worth stealing inside."

"I was more worried about someone actually taking it, not just breaking into it."

"Well as you can see, no one took it. I think you're starting to develop an unhealthy relationship with this old beast. Don't make me separate you two."

"Hilarious. Really. Maybe when all of this is over with, we can try getting you into the stand-up comedy circuit. You'll fare well with the coma patients, since they'll be the only ones who'd tolerate you. Now shut up and get in the truck, old man."

"Don't tell me to shut up. I still owe ya one, remember? I have no worries about making it hurt."

Wil closed his eyes and got in. Seatbelts were buckled, engine was turned over, and the radio turned on. Gramps made sure to switch it back to easy listening. Ten minutes down the highway, a putrid smell filled the cab.

"Oh for the love of all that's good in the world," Wil said, winding down his window. "What did I tell you about that stupid Loaded Breakfast? Roll your window down."

Gramps was already unwinding before the order was made. "That wasn't me."

"Well it wasn't me, and there's only two of us in here."

"Son, if I'd let that one go I'da claimed it. And most likely asked to stop to clear things out."

Wil frowned. "Maybe someone hit a skunk."

"Nah. That smell is inside the truck because it got better when we opened the windows."

"*Gah!* That's just brutal! Did you take your shoes off or something?"

"Sorry, son, but you're the room clearer in the foot odor department."

Wil put his finger under his nose. "I have to figure out what that is or I'm not going to make it to the next stop. It smells like—"

"Puke," a tiny voice came from the backseat. "I'm sorry."

Chapter Five

Wil darted his eyes to the rearview mirror. Dakota sat in the middle of the backseat.

"Holy crap!" He slammed on the breaks so hard he veered off onto the highway shoulder.

Gramps jumped in his seat. "Pull over here and put the flashers on."

Wil regained control of the truck and slowed down. He put it into park and turned on the warning lights. Then both he and Gramps scrambled out of their seats and opened up the back doors.

There was Dakota, pale and breathing hard. Her blonde hair was matted to her head with sweat, and she held a plastic bag from their earlier stop in her lap.

Well, Wil thought. *At least she had the courtesy and common sense to find something to puke into.*

"Dakota!" Wil shouted so loud his voice cracked. "What are you doing back there? You almost got us killed!"

"Take it easy, son," Gramps said. "Can't ya see she's scared and sick?" Gramps got into the backseat beside the girl. "Are you okay, young lady? Are you feeling any better?"

The girl nodded weakly. "I guess my tummy didn't like all the pop I had for lunch. Maybe I should have eaten something."

"You mean you didn't have any lunch?" Wil squinted. Not that he was surprised, considering the attitude of her caregivers.

"No. I wanted grilled cheese and fries but Aunt Vanessa says I'm too fat to have stuff like that so I had to have a salad. I didn't want salad, so I didn't eat anything."

Wil shook his head. *Really?* Dakota was one of the tiniest kids Wil had ever seen. And Aunt Vanessa wasn't exactly a lightweight. *She* could stand to lay off the fries. His stomach felt like someone had punched through his gut and twisted it, remembering that Aunt Vanessa and Uncle Frank each had a steak dinner with all the fixings, plus dessert.

"Well, if I'd known that I would have sent you your grilled cheese too. Here. Let me take that from you."

While Wil took the plastic bag from her lap and tied it up, Gramps took a face towel from his bag and soaked it with cold bottled water from the cooler. "Here ya go, kiddo. Wipe your face off and take a drink of this. Then you, me, and Wil here should have a chat."

Fortunately they'd stopped right by a roadside garbage can. Repressing a gag at the thought of the plastic bag's contents, he turfed it into the can, hearing an echoed splat when it hit the bottom. He faced the truck, seeing the tops of Gramps' and Dakota's heads. He was pretty sure the extra passenger wasn't part of Gramps' journey itinerary.

Gramps shuffled back over and sat on the other side of Dakota, leaving the two doors open to air out the smell. "Okay, Dakota. Are you ready to tell us what's going on?"

The girl lowered her head until her chin was tucked into her chest, her eyes glistening with tears.

Gramps and Wil looked at each other. "Okay, then," the old man said. "Why don't we just start with why you snuck into our truck?"

Dakota shot Wil a side-glance. "Well, you were so nice to me at the restaurant. Nobody ever did that stuff for me. Well, my Mama did but..." She stopped and sniffed. "I told my aunt and uncle that I had to go pee. I don't even know if they heard me, but I just went anyway. Then I went outside. I saw you drive in so I knew where your truck was. I was going to come back in, I swear. But when the back door opened up, well, I just got in. I know it was wrong but by the time I thought to get out, you were coming out and started up the engine. I got worried, my tummy felt yucky then, well... you know..."

"It's okay," Wil said, shifting his position so he faced her. "But won't your aunt and uncle be worried about you? I mean, even if they weren't acting very nice, they'll still wonder what happened to you, right?"

Dakota lifted her head up to face him. "I doubt it. Maybe if they run out of money."

Wil frowned. "What do you mean?"

"My dad left my mom when I was a baby. I don't know why. My mom never told me. Things were going okay, then my mom got sick with cancer. She couldn't take care of me like she used to. And because she had no one to help us, my dad came back and took me. My dad is fun and everything but, well, he doesn't always do nice things. He had to go to jail and that's why I'm staying with my aunt and uncle. Uncle Frank is my dad's brother, but he's even less nice than my dad."

Questions bombarded Wil's head, but he knew from experience that kids could only handle so much interrogation under normal circumstances, never mind when there were extra-crappy things going on. "Where is your mom right now?"

"Regina," she said, tears spilling down her cheeks. "I'm not allowed to talk to her, so I don't even know if she's okay."

"What do you mean you aren't allowed to talk to her?" Gramps handed the girl a tissue.

Dakota shrugged. "Daddy's rule. I heard him telling Uncle Frank during a jail visit that if he finds out I talked to Mama, he'd hurt Frank something awful and take away all the money he gives him to take care of me."

Wil's heart ached. "Does your mom have friends in Regina? Is someone helping her?"

The girl seemed to brighten a bit. "Oh yes. Auntie Kara. She's not really my aunt, but her and Mama are best friends and she's there all the time. Or, at least, she was while I was there. But I guess because Auntie Kara isn't my real family, they wouldn't let me stay with her. That's why I had to go stay with Daddy."

Thank God the mom isn't alone, especially when going through cancer.

"Okay, Dakota. I know we're asking you a whole bunch of questions, but we sorta need to know what's happening so we know what to do. You said your dad isn't always nice. Is that why he's in jail?"

Dakota nodded, wringing her tissue.

"Do you know what he did?"

She didn't answer but hugged herself.

Gramps made a cutting motion across his neck with his finger. Wil took it as a hint to stop.

"Look, we want to help you out here, kid. But me and Wil just aren't sure what to do. See, we could get into a ton of trouble taking you with us. We aren't allowed to just take you without your family's permission. You know, we'd love to take you up to see your mom. We're goin' that way anyway. But your aunt and uncle back there, or your dad, well, they're sort of the bosses, you know? The only way we can get in the middle of all of this is if something bad is going on or if someone is hurting you. Know what I mean? Otherwise, we're just gonna have to take you back to the restaurant. Your family might be worried to death."

Dakota sat up and grabbed Gramps' arm. "Oh please

don't take me back. Please? I'll tell you whatever you want to know. They don't care about me. All they care about is the money they get to take care of me. And you know what? That isn't even for them. It's to help me, and I don't even get anything. They get all this new stuff, like clothes and jewelry, and I don't get a thing. And my stupid dad only sent me to them because he was worried I'm gonna talk to someone about..." Dakota stopped, her eyes widening. She put her hands over her mouth.

"About what, kid?" Gramps asked, putting his hand over hers.

Dakota shook her head, crying even harder. "I can't tell you. I can't. They'll hurt my mom if I say anything. And they said they'd come find me if I tried getting away. Oh no. What did I do? Now they'll hurt you too."

She cried inconsolably. Wil put his arm around her, pulling her into his chest. He looked at Gramps, who was rubbing his chin. *Oh no*, he thought. *I know that look.* "Gramps? No. We can't..."

Gramps waved at Wil again. "What did you say your last name was, kid?"

"R-R-Rossi," she sputtered out between sobs.

"Did your mom always live in Regina? Did she ever say she lived anywhere else?"

Wil wasn't sure what any of that had to do with what was going on, but he kept his mouth shut and rubbed Dakota's arm. She seemed to settle down enough to answer Gramps.

"Well, I remember her telling me stories about her and Auntie Kara being in Winnipeg. Is that what you mean?"

Gramps nodded and patted the girl's leg. "Yes. That's what I meant, good girl. Okay, you lay down here and take 'er easy for a spell. Me and Wil here just gotta talk for a minute."

Wil gingerly took his arm out from under Dakota then laid her down on the backseat. He and Gramps shut the back doors and walked around to the front of the car.

"I know exactly what's brewing in your head, old man," Wil said, crossing his arms across his chest. "There is no way I'm getting involved in... whatever is going on here."

Gramps put a finger to his lips. "Keep your voice down, boy. Haven't I raised you to always do what's right even if the odds stacked up are higher than you can see over?"

"Uh, yeah. But that has to do with standing up for myself or choosing what I want to do in life. I didn't think it included taking on Uncle Frank and what I'm assuming to be some sort of Mafia thing. We have to take this girl back, Gramps. My gut is telling me this goes way deeper than them not letting her have a stupid grilled cheese sandwich."

Gramps reached up and gripped Wil's arm. "Listen, I need you to trust me on this, okay? I gotta hunch about the situation. Let's just take her up to the next stop where I can use a phone, then we'll sort out what to do next."

Wil grabbed his cell from his belt. The battery was dead. He made a mental note to hook it up to the car charger. He put his hands on top of his head and breathed out sharply. "You heard her say that they're going to come looking for her, right?"

"Yeah."

"Well, what happens if they do?"

"So what?"

Wil moved his hands to his hips. "'So what?' Are you kidding me? Uncle Frank looks like one of those dudes from the *Godfather* movies. He's probably packing some heat somewhere. And the way she described her dad, he's probably even worse. What do we have? Your biting wit? That's only going to get us killed."

Gramps sputtered out a raspberry. "You sporting panties under those jeans, boy? I've never known you to be scared of anything before. Even if you knew you had to come home to me, you did what you thought needed to be done. This little girl needs us, and we're gonna do what we can. Period."

With that, Gramps shuffled back to the truck and got back in, slamming his door hard enough to give it a good shake. Wil stood there, his hands still on his hips, staring out at the bright yellow mustard seed field.

Panties or not, I'd like to stay alive a little longer.

After several minutes, he sighed deeply then got back into the driver's seat. He looked at Dakota in the rearview mirror. Her shoulder rose and fell as she slept soundly.

He started the truck back up and then pulled his seatbelt across his chest. The two men sat there, the vehicle vibrating as the engine grumbled.

"Well?" Gramps asked.

"Well, you'd better know kung fu or something, old man, because we're going to need some sort of secret weapon."

Gramps punched Wil in the shoulder. "Good boy."

"And stop hitting me. Save it for Uncle Frank."

They drove on to Brandon in silence. It would only be another couple of hours.

This is way more excitement than I really wanted on this trip, he thought. *What else could possibly happen?*

****

Gramps managed to stay awake for the entire hour and forty-five-minute drive. Thank goodness they had the radio. Music seemed to fill in the quiet gap as well as keep Wil's mind from racing out of control. Gramps tapped his fingers on the armrest, whether there was a rhythm or not, staring out of the front window.

Wil chose a coffee shop just inside the city of Brandon so they could make a quick escape if need be. *Great,* he thought, pulling into a parking spot right in front of the café. *I've become more paranoid than a killer on the run.*

Bad choice of words.

He shut the engine off. "Well? What's the plan?"

Gramps rubbed the white stubble on his chin with his palm. "Why don't you take the girl into the coffee shop, and I'll meet you in there in a few minutes. I'm betting she's hungry after losing what little she ate earlier." He pulled Wil's cell phone from the charger sticking out from the cigarette lighter then said, "Got a call or two to make."

"Well, by all means, please feel free to use my cell phone for all your calling needs."

"And whose name is on the contract givin' you permission to have one of these things?

"And who pays the bill?"

The two men glared at each other. Then Wil released a deep breath. "Fine. Just don't go calling Australia or something, okay? I only have so many minutes and we need the phone in case of emergencies."

"Well, maybe one will come up," Gramps cranked, pushing the button on the side of the phone with his thumb to turn it on.

"Do you guys always argue like this?" Dakota's voice broke in. "It's funny."

"Yeah, hilarious," Wil muttered under his breath, giving Gramps' thigh a light tap with the back of his hand. "I'll take her in. Don't suck up all of our minutes, old man."

"Hmph," Gramps sputtered. "Order me an extra large coffee and a piece of apple pie. And if you get 'em to slap a scoop of ice cream on top, I won't complain."

"Well, by all means. We'll be sure to do that, then, so Dakota and I can spare ourselves a headache right off the bat."

Dakota giggled from behind her hands.

"Okay, kiddo. Let's go get us a snack," Wil said, looking in the rearview mirror at her.

The girl slid across the back seat and got out of the door on Wil's side of the truck. Wil opened his door but before getting out, he leaned over to Gramps and said, "I shouldn't be worried about what you're doing right now, should I?"

Gramps waved him away, already pushing numbers into the phone keypad. "You just get in there and take care of that girl. I have a hunch I need to follow. I'll explain everything when I come in."

Wil nodded then got out. Dakota sat on the front steps waiting, hugging her knees close to her chest. He slammed the door then took the spot beside her. "Everything will be okay," he said. "One way or another, we'll figure things out."

"I'm not really worried about it," she said. The breeze blew her strawberry blonde hair over her shoulders. "I'm not scared either. I just want to find my mom. And I really hope they don't come to find me before I get to."

Wil creased his brow. "By 'they' do you mean your Uncle Frank and your aunt? Or your dad?"

"Any of them. If my dad finds out what happened, he's going to be super mad. Trust me. For some reason, he just doesn't want me to go. I don't get that either because it's not like he ever played with me. Or spent time with me. He just got other people to."

She rested her chin on her arms. Wil had an urge to run his hand down her hair or some other comforting gesture parent-type people did. But he didn't want to come across as weird, so he shook the feeling off.

"Look, why don't we just go inside and wait for Gramps? I'll bet you're pretty hungry. Besides, if his pie and coffee aren't waiting for him when he's done, he's going to give me a firm talking to."

Dakota smiled. "Okay." She stood up then looked up at Wil meekly. "Can I have a grilled cheese?"

"Sure."

"With french fries?"

"Of course."

"And a chocolate milkshake? And pie too, just like Gramps?"

"That's one huge pile of food. Can you eat all that?"

She nodded, her eyes widened. "Oh yes. I'm super-duper hungry."

Wil squinted down at her, rubbing his lip between his index finger and his thumb. "Hmm. Well, okay. But you better not puke in my shiny, clean truck again, or I'll make you walk."

"Deal." She laughed and held out her hand.

"Deal." He shook her hand, then they got up and walked to the door.

Wil opened it for her but before going in, he looked back at Gramps, who was still on the phone. The look of concern on his face made Wil's stomach explode with nerves. He chewed the inside of his lower lip and walked into the café behind Dakota.

The two sat at a booth by the window facing the parking lot. Wil ordered for everyone, telling the waitress not to bring the pie over until Gramps came in so there'd be no choice words about melted ice cream. After ten minutes, Dakota's meal of champions was brought to the table just as Gramps came in and joined them.

"Holy mackerel!" He opened his eyes wide and slapped his forehead. "That's more food than this boy eats in an entire day! You really gonna eat all that?"

"You just watch me," Dakota said with a smile that lit up her entire freckled face. As she squirted a huge blob of ketchup beside her sandwich, Wil waved at the waitress, signaling her to bring over Gramps' pie. Still feeling full from his lunch, Wil nursed a coffee.

"So?"

Gramps put his hands around his coffee mug. "Dang it. This is lukewarm. Why in Fort Knox would you tell them to pour me coffee before I got in here?" He leaned across the table to Dakota, nodding his head at Wil. "Not the sharpest tack in the box, ya know?" Then he winked, triggering a giggle from the little girl.

"Funny. Just get her to warm it up when she brings you the pie," Wil said, irritated by the obvious avoidance of his question. "Are you going to fill me in or what?"

The waitress brought over the pie, with two scoops of ice cream, and a fresh cup of coffee. "See, now that's service."

"Gramps!"

Dakota jumped at the sudden outburst, looked at both men then stuffed the rest of her first half of the sandwich into her mouth. Gramps gave Wil a look that could have melted the ice cream on his plate into a creamy puddle. "Listen, I'm gonna take this boy over to the condiments table with me and teach him some manners. You stay here and keep eating. We'll just be right there, okay?" Gramps pointed to the counter twelve feet away.

The girl nodded then sucked on the straw in her milkshake. The two men walked over to the counter and sat on a couple of stools set up in front of it. Wil turned his around to face Dakota then leaned back.

"Let's get something straight right now," Gramps said, poking Wil in the arm with a finger. "I know you don't have experience dealing with younger kids, but you can't just be blurting things out like that. Especially not for a kid like her who has had some rough patches to deal with. I may seem rough around the edges, but I know kids."

Yeah. Edges like a puffer fish, Wil thought.

"I'm sorry. And I'll apologize to her too. I'm just a little stressed here, you know? Did you get a hold of whoever you were trying to call?"

"Yup."

Wil waited while Gramps topped his coffee with creamer, blew into his cup, and slurped.

"Well?"

"Well, things are a little more complicated than I thought. Something about Dakota's story just ate at my gut, like it was familiar, you know? Then when she told me her last name, it all hit me like a ton of bricks."

He paused to take another sip of Joe before going on. "Your Aunt Audrey had this friend named Sophia. Sweetest little thing, so shy and quiet. Nice girl. Anyway, she and your aunt were pretty tight. Spent all their time together. Our families got close on account of the girls. Sophia's dad, Tom, was going through a rough patch with his grocery store. Had to take out a loan but the banks wouldn't go near him. Let's just say he made the mistake of turning to a well-known underground lending business."

"You mean like a loan shark?"

"Somethin' like that. But this guy was really bad news. Did stuff I don't even wanna tell ya about. These young hoodlums started coming around, harassing poor Tom and his wife, even following our girls to school. They looked just like that Fuzzy guy from that TV show your dad used to like on reruns. You remember? That feller that stuck his thumbs up all the time."

Wil looked at Gramps like he had three heads, repressing a smile. "You mean Fonzie?"

"Fuzzy, Fonzie, whatever. Hoodlum's a hoodlum. Anyhow, things got so bad, they all had to leave town. Moved out to a small town in Saskatchewan. Unfortunately, they were found and…"

Gramps shook his head, gripping his mug so tightly his knuckles turned white. "House burned to the ground with the family inside, and anything else that could bring in a nickel was taken. Course it was all believed to be an accident. Only Sophia survived because she wasn't home when it all happened. She stayed in contact with your aunt. Guess she grew up, moved on, and found a guy she thought was Mr. Right. Only he turned out to be anything but."

Wil was as intrigued as if he watched a big-budget suspense movie. "What happened?"

"Long story short—"

"Too late."

Gramps clicked his tongue. "Just zip it, you. So, Sophia met some oil slick guy, and he wooed her relentlessly. Gave her gifts, took her places, the whole nine yards. Well, she ended up marrying the guy only to find out that not only was he into the same bad business that her dad got involved with years earlier, but that her hubby was one of the sons of the no-good loan shark he borrowed money from."

"So essentially, she married into the family who killed her own family? And how did she not know about that before she married the jerk?"

"Don't know." Gramps shrugged, shoving his cup across the counter and motioning for a refill. "It's not like they make a public announcement about things. That's not the worst of it. Sophia had two sons with the guy. The older one's name is Antonio, and her younger boy is Frank."

The coffee Wil had had bubbled up in the pit of his stomach. *I don't like where this is going.*

"Antonio hooked up with some young thing in Regina and she got pregnant. Guess they never got married. She refused. But he helped take care of her and the baby. Seems that he bought multi-million dollar life insurance policies out on him and the mom, guess so the kid would be well taken care of in case either of them... died. And guess who the beneficiary is of those policies?"

Wil swallowed hard, switching his gaze over to Dakota, who was savoring her french fries.

"You got it." Gramps leaned in closer to Wil. "Not only that, but the kid also has millions set up for her in trust funds and other investments so her school and everything will be covered for her for the rest of her life. So, what we got here is a little girl with a deep connection to one of the oldest and most dangerous Mob families in Western Canada. She's worth millions and nobody gives a blast about her beyond the loot. Except her mama."

"And something tells me some of those nobodies will do anything to get their hands on her." Wil's mouth was drier than sand. He tried wrapping his head around the mountain of information Gramps had just dumped on him. "Well, it makes sense why Uncle Frank has such a vested interest in her. Does Dakota have access to the money?"

Gramps shook his head. "No. Not 'til she turns eighteen. Guess that's a good thing, in a way. No one can get their grubby hands on it for a while. She said that Frank guy is paid to care for her. Guess maybe he'll get a share of the loot once she's of age."

"Okay. The only thing I'm a bit confused about this kid's mom. Isn't she sick or something? I didn't think life insurance policies covered when a person is dying. Isn't that supposed to be for accidental death or whatever?"

"Son, do I look like an insurance agent to you? What do I know about that sorta stuff? All I know is that we're dealing with the Mob here. They can make almost anything happen if they got the right people on their side."

Wil frowned. "And when did you become such an expert on illegal operations?"

"Never you mind. The most important thing right now is getting this kid to her mama."

"Oh is *that* all?" Wil said, slapping his thigh. "Well, good grief. Let's get going. C'mon. And I won't worry about the Mob hunting us down like dogs or that we have no idea where to even find Dakota's mom or even if she's still alive. Gramps? Are you *insane*? We've gotten into this far enough. I say we should just take her to the local authorities where she'll be safe and—"

"And how do you know that the local authorities aren't working with them?"

Wil put his palms up to Gramps. "Okay. Clearly you have watched way too many of these gangster-type movies, and your imagination is going bizerko. Things like that don't really happen, Gramps."

"Yeah they do, son."

"No, they don't."

"Trust me, they do."

"Again, I'm going to ask how you know. You're really freaking me out here. It's not bad enough with all the talk about the Mob but for Pete's sake, Gramps. This girl's grandparents were killed. On purpose. By the very people we're hiding her from. You can *not* be serious about continuing with this."

Gramps swung his legs around, coffee in hand then got off his chair. "Your aunt told me that once Sophia's husband died and the boys took over the family business, it went even darker than it had been before. Wasn't just knee-breaking loan sharks, but more into stuff like prostitution, drugs, and other crap I don't even wanna bring up."

He waved his fingers at Wil to follow him and headed back in the direction of the table. "Sophia took off, found Casey, the kid's mom, and got her and Dakota into protective custody. They were doin' great too, until Casey got sick. Then Antonio's lackeys found her in the hospital and led him straight to the girl. Sophia got Casey hidden again, but they've been trying to find Dakota here to bring her back. Once they have her, Antonio can't do a thing. Then the money will be all Dakota's. He knows authorities are waiting to take him away. Doesn't mean he isn't gonna try."

The bubbling in Wil's stomach turned into an all-out burning sensation. "This was supposed to have been some stupid road trip you wanted to take me on to show me stuff about my past. How did it turn into an adventure that Pacino would want to participate in?"

"I know where Casey lives, son," Gramps said just before sitting back down. "If we can find our way out there, everything else is taken care of. Then we can get back on course. Besides, you're learning about your past. You just don't realize it yet."

Wil dropped down beside Dakota, who was slurping up the last of her milkshake. All that was left on her plate where four crusts and a few fries. "Oh thank you so much for that. It was the best thing I've ever eaten in so, so long!"

She leaned into Wil's torso and squeezed him with such force, he grunted from the pressure. He looked at Gramps, who had tears in his eyes, then put his arm around the girl, pulling her closer. "Hey, no worries. As long as you enjoyed it."

He rubbed Dakota's arm with his palm then nodded at Gramps.

Gramps nodded back then swigged back the rest of his coffee. "Right, then. We got a lot of road to cover before it's time for bed. Let's get to it."

"What? You aren't going to eat that pie after grouching about it?"

"I ain't eating that now. The ice cream's all melted. It's like pie soup. That's more disgusting than those Mexican hoagie things you bring home from work some days."

Wil shot Gramps a deadpan stare then grabbed the bill.

I'm dealing with two children here, he thought. *And the younger one is better behaved.*

He shoved twenty-five dollars under the receipt and dug out three twoonies, throwing them on top of it, and followed the dynamic duo out the door. Watching Gramps and Dakota "race" to the car, the side of his mouth tugged up into a half-smile. It seemed the further they went along this little adventure, the deeper the mysteries became.

What else you got in store for me, old man?
And will I make it 'til the end?

Chapter Six

With no formal plan of where they'd be stopping next, Wil turned back onto the Trans-Canada going west. Even though he had no clue where they were going, he figured they'd end up somewhere in Saskatchewan, so it was best to stay on in that direction.

After half an hour of listening to the sound of the tires whizzing along the tar road, Gramps finally said, "Let's head up to Whitewood and stay there for the night. Cover as much road as we can in the next couple of hours." He twisted his arm to check his watch. "Should be well past seven by then. We can have a late supper and get our girl to bed."

Our girl. "Sounds like she's growing on ya, you big softy." Wil smiled.

Gramps strained to see behind him in the mirror on his visor. Dakota was fast asleep. "It doesn't matter who a kid is or where she's from, she should be able to enjoy just bein' a kid. It really ticks me off when kids, animals, or other innocent people are treated so bad. It ain't fair."

"Life can be unfair. That's what you always taught me."

"Yeah. I also taught you that it's okay to let it kick you in the butt, but it's not okay to let it keep you down. And I remember teaching you that if you find others that need help along the way, you should always stop and do what you can. What goes around comes around, boy."

"Why are you getting all philosophical and Confucius-like on me? It's creepy."

"See? *This* is why my butt gets burned so bad with you. Everything is a joke with you, isn't it? Somewhere along this trip, I'm gonna teach ya to be a little more serious about things."

"And I'm hoping at some point to teach you that life doesn't always have to be so serious and rigid. C'mon, lighten up. You're so uptight you'll start shooting diamonds out of your butt."

Dakota's hiccup laugh exploded from the backseat. "Diamonds out of his butt. Ha ha ha! That's so funny!"

"Great. Now you woke up the kid. Nice going."

Gramps glared at Wil. "*Me?* Who's over there talking about butts, diamonds, and some confusion person."

That got Wil going. "It's Confucius. He was one of the greatest Chinese philosophers of all time. He—"

"Whatever. Any guy whose name hints to confusing people with his words ain't someone I wanna learn about. I got my own theories on life."

"Yeah. Saints help us all."

After her short nap, Dakota seemed to perk up a bit. The three passengers engaged in a bit of chitchat, then Dakota asked what felt like an endless list of questions for a good twenty minutes. When Wil couldn't answer one more 'why' or 'what if', he suggested they all play a rousing game of I Spy. That seemed to do the trick until they got to the Saskatchewan/Manitoba border. Then all there was to spy were wheat and mustard seed fields, hay bales and the occasional cow or horse. That's when Gramps thought it would be a fun idea to sing "A Hundred Bottles of Pop on the

Wall."

Perfect, Wil thought. *Nothing like listening to a repetitive song over-the-top-loud, and off-key for the next hour.*

While the other two passengers sang, Wil's mind wandered back to road trips to the summer cabin with his parents. The rides had never been boring. His mom had always found a way to make the ride fun with stories, singing, or the same I Spy game he'd suggested. Back then, there hadn't been any DVD players in the car or MP3 players or cell phones to surf the web or to text or even play mini-video games. It was all about creating fun... as a family.

His favorite time had been when his dad had played a prank on his mom on the one and only time she had dared to fall asleep. He and his dad had planned it for every road trip, but the trick had never happened since Mom, being in charge of the entertainment, had always stayed awake. That time they had finally gotten their chance.

"Hey, Wil," his father had said in a loud whisper, looking at him in the rearview mirror. "Here comes a semi. When he pulls up beside us, do what I showed you."

Wil had leaned over the front seat to peek at his mom: out cold asleep. He gave his dad the thumbs-up in the mirror then turned to see how close the truck was. The front grill of the road monster was almost at the trunk of their car.

Wil remembered how their tiny car had trembled from the force of the huge truck trying to pass them on the highway. The screaming of its massive wheels spinning against the road sounded pretty close to a passenger airplane getting ready for takeoff. The closer the semi had gotten, the harder their car vibrated as his dad had tried to keep the car from veering off onto the shoulder.

As the truck inched up beside their car, Wil had moved right against his window, straining to look up at the driver. The wheels had seemed like inches away from them.

"Now!" his dad had shouted as the two vehicles drove

neck-in-neck.

On cue, Wil had pumped his arm up and down, similar to the motion of pulling down on a crane. The driver looked down at Wil, pointed his finger at him, then pulled down on the horn.

Three long honks blasted out, shocking his mother out of her deep sleep. She had screamed, throwing one arm up against the roof of the car while the other whacked against her window.

His father had burst into laughter. "Oh no. Did we wake you up?"

"You crazy man," his mother had said, giving him a playful slap on the forearm. "Are you trying to give me a heart attack or something? Look. You gave me such a start, I kicked over the cooler."

"That'll teach you to fall asleep with two boys in the car who need constant entertainment."

"Oh, just shut up and drive, Mr. Carter."

The three of them had laughed until tears flowed and sides ached. Those times with his parents had been so special. He only wished he'd realized then what treasures even those silly moments would be later on. As his parents' laughter echoed in his head, Wil was yanked out of his daydream by his grandfather's urgent orders.

"There's a roadside bathroom just up ahead. Dakota just said she has to pee, not that you heard her."

Instead of firing out his usual sarcastic retort, Wil chose to ignore him and pulled over so Dakota could use the bathroom. When the girl disappeared into the girls' side of the luxury outhouse, Gramps unbuckled his seatbelt and got out of the truck for a stretch. Wil stayed in his seat, leaning over the steering wheel.

Gramps leaned into his car window. "You okay?"

"Yeah," Wil said, flicking the old man a glance. He rested his chin on his forearm. "Just thinking…"

"Trip making you think about your parents, huh?"

Wil stayed quiet.

"Thought so. Good. About time you and me started talking about them again."

Wil leaned back in his seat. He pushed against the steering wheel with his palms. "I don't really want to talk about them right now. I'm fine."

"You keep people in your heart by talking about them, son. I know it hurts, but you can't stop talking or your heart will close and your memories will fade. I told you that."

"You told me that when I was six, Gramps," Wil said. He turned his head and looked out of his window. He watched one lone cloud drifting by. "You also told me they'd always be here for me, even if I can't see them. I'm not a kid anymore. I don't need the fairy tales."

"Land sakes, boy. At what point did you become so hard-hearted? I might be a bit crusty, and you weren't raised by your parents, but I sure as guns made sure you were surrounded with enough love not to be so jaded."

Wil watched the cloud as it spread out a bit, looking a bit like a cotton ball that had been pulled apart. He turned back to look at Gramps, who stared down at him.

Why haven't I noticed how much he looks like Dad? The eyes… that crease between his eyebrows when he's concentrating hard on something…

The young man shook his head. "I'm not hard-hearted. Or jaded. Just tired, I guess. And sick of all these surprises that keep popping up."

"Mmm-hmm," Gramps nodded his head, seeming to accept the subtle change in subject. "You want me to drive to Whitewood? It's only twenty minutes."

"Really, Gramps? I hate to remind you of this yet again but you have no license, remember?"

"How could I forget when you keep bringing it up? Besides, who in blazes is going to catch us out here?"

"With how things have been going on this trip so far, the entire RCMP force would come down on us. And knowing how slow you drive, it wouldn't be much of a chase."

Gramps sputtered. "Nice to see your spit and fire is back. Need to use the bathroom?"

"Well, as touching as your concern for my bladder needs are, I'm fine, thanks."

"Didn't mean the bladder. Just thought you might wanna clear your system out so we don't have to deal with any more of your cranks. An empty system makes for a happier disposition, don't ya know?"

Wil slapped his forehead. "Well, you could have told me that from the get-go. I'd have made sure you stocked up on prunes and then stopped every ten minutes for you."

Dakota's laughter from behind Gramps stopped the banter. The old man moved out of the way and Wil saw her doubled over in hysterics.

"You guys are *so* hilarious! The way you say stuff makes me laugh so hard I could puke."

Wil sighed. "Yeah, well. I think we've had enough puking for today. Everyone get back in and buckle up. We don't have much further to go, and I'd like to get this part over with."

He turned the key in the ignition once Gramps and Dakota got back in and then they were on their way. As Wil pulled back onto the highway, Gramps turned the radio up, then leaned closer to him, his voice just above a whisper. "You notice that red SUV back there?"

Wil glanced in the rearview mirror. "Barely. Why?"

"I've seen it following us for a while."

"Gee, how odd to see another car on the highway. Gramps, I think you're getting paranoid."

"Oh, put a sock in it, boy! I'm the least paranoid guy you know. Besides, I saw the same truck in the parking lot back at Perry's. And a vehicle that was just driving along would have passed us when we stopped at the loo."

Wil looked back up at the rearview mirror, noticing the SUV wasn't getting any closer. Almost as if it was keeping a safe distance to keep an eye on them. His heart picked up a faster pace.

"Well, that's just great. Now that I notice it, I'm crapping myself."

"Told you to use the bathroom back there."

"If you even start saying that stupid expression about my disposition, I'm going to have to slug you." He pushed on the gas pedal a little harder and flicked another look at the mirror. "Do you think that's Uncle Psycho?"

Gramps grunted. "Don't know. Could be. Let's just focus on watching for the turn off to Whitewood and finding us a place to stay for the night. You let me worry about meeting up with that punk."

Great, Wil thought. *Now he thinks he's Clint Eastwood. We are so pooched.*

Chapter Seven

Wil pulled into the first respectable-looking motel they came to. It was clean, had an ice cooler out front, and a pool. It was attached to a small strip mall with a hair salon, a café, a souvenir store, a drug store, and a pub on the other end. For some reason, the motel gave Wil the feel that Norman Bates was about to pop out from behind somewhere in his mother's wig and dress. But Gramps assured him that he was just being paranoid, as usual.

He lost the argument over who'd pay for the room, so while Gramps grilled the desk clerk about what was included in the fee, Wil took Dakota out the back door to check out the pool.

The pool area was surrounded by a twelve-foot high metal fence with some sort of sheer, black, rubbery cover stuck against it. Wil guessed it was to offer pool patrons a bit of privacy from people driving past.

They walked up to the gate, and Wil noted the huge padlock hanging from the handle. Wil got closer to the fence, trying to peer through the metal links and plastic cover. There was a shallow kid's pool on one end and a hot tub on the other. Considering the two-star look of the motel, the pool seemed to be well-maintained and clear. With the typical Saskatchewan summer weather still a sweltering 35 above, even at seven o'clock at night, the deep blue water looked inviting.

"Hey! Maybe we can go for a dip tomorrow morning before heading back out," Wil said.

Dakota pouted. "But I don't have a bathing suit."

"Me neither. But I think I saw some suits in the window of that store down the way. Let's go see. Maybe we can find something in the old man's size and make him join us."

They both jumped at the sudden snort from behind them. "It'll be a snowy day in Haiti before you'll get me in some trunks again. But why don't we stop by that store on our way to get a bedtime snack at the restaurant?"

"Chicken," Wil said. "C'mon. You still got the legs for it. Maybe they even have one of those full late-1800-style ones for ya. The ladies will be all over you."

"Shut it and let's go, smart rear. We should get the little lady here back as soon as possible for some shut-eye. Been a long day."

Wil repressed a snicker, waved Dakota ahead of him with Gramps, and followed them back to the motel lobby. The trio cut through the motel to get to the sidewalk out front then up the strip mall to the store.

The storeowner was about to close up but allowed them to come in, flipping the 'Closed' sign behind them. Dakota found a bright blue one-piece with different colored palm trees all over it. Wil chose a pair of white trunks with red maple leafs all over them.

"How patriotic of you, boy," Gramps smirked. "I hope for everyone's sake those aren't see-through when they get wet."

"I think there's enough leaf clusters in the right spots that I won't embarrass myself."

Wil took Dakota's bathing suit and put it on the cashier's

counter with his trunks. As he reached in his back pocket to pull out his wallet, Gramps grabbed his wrist. "This one's on me, son."

"I'm confused. First the motel room and now this? What's with all the generosity all of a sudden? It's almost painful for you to spend money most of the time, even for gifts. What's up? You find a money tree you're not telling us about?"

Gramps shook his head. "Can't I just do something nice without the Spanish Inquisition? I just want to, all right? Done."

"You'd better watch it, mister. Folks might start thinking your cranky, tough guy stuff is all just an act."

"Hmph. Just shut up, take the kid outside and wait for me."

Wil put his arm around Dakota and guided her outside. While they talked about what they'd have at the restaurant, something caught Wil's eye on the main road: the red SUV. The windows were blacked out, preventing Wil from seeing who was in the vehicle. It seemed to slow down as it drove past them, then it took off around the corner.

A slosh of bile gurgled in Wil's stomach as he tried his best to maintain his cool in front of Dakota. He felt a slap on his back that almost made him jump out of his skin.

"What's wrong with you, boy?" Gramps creased his brow and peered up at Wil over his glasses. "You look like you've seen a ghost."

Wil stared in the direction of where the truck had turned.

Not a ghost, but definitely not someone I want to see anytime soon.

"Well, if you're going to just stand there staring off into nowhere land, at least close your mouth. Bugs are out now. Besides, you aren't exactly making yourself look any smarter."

Dakota burst into laughter.

Wil shifted his eyes down at Gramps. "Now who's being a smart rear?"

"My butt is smarter than you look at the moment." Gramps turned and waved for the other two to follow him. "Let's move on up to the restaurant, already. I need my nighttime coffee."

On the short walk up to the café, Wil looked over his shoulder a dozen times. He darted his eyes from one side of the street to the other ahead of them. *Thanks for the paranoia, old man*, he thought. He didn't feel any better in the café.

They sat at a booth close to the front, right next to the window. Every time a car drove by, Wil's heart picked up its pace.

Just how did this happen? he thought. *I could be working my easygoing job at the pharmacy then hanging out with my friends in the evenings. Spending the weekends at the beach. But, no. I allowed myself to be strong-armed into this stupid road trip that's turning more and more into an episode of a really bad detective show. If I make it through this, I'm putting Gramps in an old folks' home for someone else to deal with.*

Wil was yanked out of his thoughts by an elbow to the ribs. "Wil! Snap out of it. This lovely lady has more important things to do than to wait for your brain and mouth to connect. Tell her what you want."

"Huh?" Wil rubbed his side. He hadn't even heard the waitress come to the table, or Dakota and Gramps ordering. "Sorry. Uh… I'll have an order of poutine and a large orange juice."

The waitress, who didn't look much younger than Gramps, gathered the menus and then yelled their order to the kitchen. Wil flicked another glance out the window.

"I need to go pee," said Dakota.

"I saw the washrooms when we came in." Gramps nodded in the direction of the door. "Go on ahead. Shouldn't be too long for our order."

Dakota scooted out of her side of the booth and shuffled off to the bathroom. Wil was relieved that they'd be able to keep a close eye on where she was, considering who was possibly out there waiting for them. Once the door to the girls' bathroom closed behind Dakota, Gramps bumped Wil with his shoulder.

"What the Sam Hill is wrong with you, boy? You're acting as jumpy as a cat in a room full of rocking chairs. Relax, will ya? You're making me uncomfortable."

"Well, excuse me. I am so sorry to be the cause of any discomfort you might be feeling. Maybe if you'd kept your crazy idea of someone following us to yourself, I would feel more relaxed."

"I told you not to worry about that."

"Yes, I know. But I am. How can I *not* worry about it? Ever seen "Scarface"? Uncle Frank sort of reminds me of Pacino in that movie. Crazy, unstable and... well... dang scary."

Gramps shook his head. "You have to trust me, boy. If anyone in that family has the dander to mess with either of us or that little girl, I'll end it. For good."

"Worry, will you please?"

"What's that?"

"Worry. Please. Because when you don't, it means you know something that I don't and that scares me more than anything Frank could do to us."

"You're getting soft, son. I think the heat is getting to you."

Before Wil had a chance to respond, the waitress slid plates in front of each of them. As she straightened her stance, Dakota sneaked around her and plunked back down in her seat. Gramps got blueberry pie *a la mode* and coffee, Dakota opted for a milkshake, while Wil got his plateful of fries and cheese curds with gravy and juice. He didn't have much of an appetite for the mountain of heart-attack-on-a-plate anymore, though.

Gramps put a forkful of pie dripping with ice cream in

his mouth then pointed at Wil's plate with his fork. "Nice bedtime snack choice. You're gonna either get nightmares or your digestive system is gonna get you back in the middle of the night. Either way, I'm not happy you'll be in the same room as me."

"Oh, what are you worried about? I'll be on a cot on the other side of the room. Thanks, by the way, for not making me sleep on the floor."

"Tried to tell the clerk to just toss an extra pillow and comforter in the corner, but she wouldn't have it. Thank her, not me."

"Nice." Wil stabbed a fry then brought it up to his mouth. Poutine was his favorite indulgence food on the planet but, for some reason, it only made him want to hurl right then. He put his fork on his plate and then leaned back. He turned his head to the right and a couple in the back corner of the café caught his eye.

They sat on the same side of the booth, sitting so close together an observer would have thought they were attached. They gazed in each other's eyes. She laughed at something the guy said, flipped her hair over her shoulder, then they kissed.

A flash of his parents drifted into his mind. They were always like that, just like honeymooners. Sitting close, hugging, stealing kisses. And he'd loved it. It had given him faith in love. And then they were gone. Forever.

A take-out container was shoved in front of him.

"Since you didn't answer the waitress, again, I thought you'd want to take your food back with us. You know, since you didn't eat any of it. There's a nuker in the room in case you want it later." Gramps squeezed Wil's forearm then slid out of the booth. "Already took care of the bill, so let's go back to the motel and get some shut-eye. We'll grab our bags from the car. I think all of us will feel better after a good sleep."

After bribing Dakota to have a shower by promising to have an early morning swim, Wil gave the girl one of his T-shirts to use as pajamas. She jumped into one of the queen-sized beds and pulled the covers up to her neck. Wil repressed a smile, seeing how tiny she looked in such a big bed.

"Aren't you going to be hot under the covers?" He sat down on the edge beside her. "It's still pretty hot out."

"Nah. I'll be okay. That air conditioner is pretty cold."

"Good point."

Wil noticed that Dakota's eyes suddenly flooded with tears.

"What's wrong? Do you need something?"

"I miss my Lamby," she said. "I forgot to bring it with me when I got into your truck at Perry's. I don't know if I can sleep without him."

Gramps gripped Wil's shoulder and said, "Well, while you two were waiting for me outside at the store, I got ya something." He passed Dakota a plastic bag with the store's logo on it.

She tugged the bag open then gasped. She looked up at Gramps, giving him a smile that lit up her whole face. Then she reached inside the bag and pulled out a small, stuffed lamb wearing a pink dress and a bow on her right ear.

"Oh my goodness. She almost looks just like Lamby! How did you know?"

Gramps shrugged. "Didn't. Just saw the sweet little thing and she had your name all over her. Maybe she can help you sleep."

Dakota scrambled out from under her covers, stood up, and wrapped her tiny arms around Gramps' neck. "Thank you so much," she whispered.

Wil watched as Gramps' expression went from one of surprise to a smile. Then the old man wrapped his arms around Dakota's torso, giving her back a few gentle rubs. "You are so welcome, my girl. Now let's get you in bed, okay? Or you won't have the strength for swimming tomorrow."

The girl scootched back under her covers, placing the

lamb on her pillow beside her head. "What about prayers?"

"You usually have a bedtime prayer you say?" Gramps adjusted her covers back under her neck.

"Oh yes. I have to. Mama said no matter where I am or where she is, I have to say my prayers."

"Well alrighty, then. Let's do it."

Wil fidgeted. He stopped saying prayers a long time ago. In all honesty, he wasn't even sure he believed in God anymore. How could a God take away a kid's parents? Or let what had happened to Dakota happen? It didn't seem right. Yeah, he'd been taught in Sunday school that God didn't make things happen, people do. Just like his aunt had told him. But still.

Dakota wound her fingers together, tucked her hands under her chin, and said, "Now I lay me down to sleep, I pray the Lord my soul to keep. If I should die before I wake, I pray the Lord my soul to take. This I ask for Jesus's sake. Amen. God bless Mama. Please keep her safe, God. And keep her healthy until I can go help her again. She really needs me, you know. God bless Uncle Frank and Auntie Vanessa, even though they can be mad sometimes."

A lump the size of a golf ball grew in Wil's throat. How could a kid pray for people who treated her so badly? He got that was what prayer was for, but even so.

Dakota continued. "And most of all, God, please bless Gramps and Wil. They are so funny and nice and they are doing good stuff. They fight a lot, but it's all okay because they love each other. I know it. Amen."

The two men shared a look for a few seconds then nodded. After everyone had washed, brushed their teeth, and gotten into their designated beds, Gramps turned the lights off.

After only a few minutes, Wil heard Dakota's deep breathing and Gramps' short, staccato-like snorts. He wished he were able to fall asleep as easily. With everything that had happened to him that day, one would think sleep would hit him a lot harder. And it was only the first day of their road trip. He sighed then rolled over.

The cot he lay on was lumpy and creaked with the slightest movement. He finally got comfortable on his back then stared out past the dirty streaks in the window into the dark night sky. There was still a hint of daylight, but the stars were already popping out.

Wil couldn't stop thinking about Dakota's prayer. He wasn't sure if Gramps knew it or not, but his mom had used to say the same one to him when he was little. They'd said it together every night until she died. For the first few weeks after he'd moved in with Gramps, he remembered saying it. He'd prayed every night for God to bring his parents back. To just give him a reason he could understand that they had to be taken away. He'd never got an answer. So he'd stopped praying.

He closed his eyes to fight the tears pooling in them. He wasn't sure what it was his grandfather was trying to teach him on their journey but so far, all he was learning was how deeply he still missed his parents. They'd never gotten to see him grow up into a man or hug him when he was hurt or scared. They hadn't met his first girlfriend or cheered him on at soccer or baseball. And they hadn't gotten to see him graduate from high school, and they would not see him off to college. They'd missed everything up to where he was right then and would miss everything after. And it hurt like tar nation.

He opened his eyes. The sky was darker, and the stars sparkled brightly around the full moon. His aunts and uncles told him that his mom and dad would always be watching over him from heaven. So did Gramps. Because he was never certain whether that could really happen, he'd made sure to be good and do right, just in case.

"Everything happens for a reason." His mother's voice

echoed in his memory. *"Good or bad, happy or sad, we are supposed to learn from every experience. We may not understand it at the time, but eventually, it all makes sense."*

His parents' accident, and their deaths, didn't make sense. It never would. But maybe if they really were up there watching over him, they would help him figure out what he was supposed to learn from the mess he, Gramps, and Dakota were in.

Good or bad... happy or sad... it will all make sense.

With the sound of snoring inside their room, and crickets and the occasional car passing by outside, Wil slowly relaxed into a motionless sleep.

****

"Wil!"

Most people were allowed to wake up on their own or were gently lulled awake with whispers or loving shakes. Even the shock of an alarm clock was gentler than being woken up to the sound of an old man's squawks.

"Wil! Boy! Get up!"

"What exactly is your problem? We've had this discussion before. Just because you like getting up at five doesn't mean everyone has to. It's not like—"

"Dakota is gone." Gramps interrupted.

Wil shot up to a sitting position. "What are you talking about? What do you mean she's gone?"

"I slipped out to get us all some grub from the restaurant, and when I came back she wasn't in her bed."

"Did you check the bathroom?"

"For the love of crumpets, boy. The place isn't that big. The bathroom is the first thing you see when you walk in. She isn't here."

Wil darted his eyes over to the top of the dresser where they'd put their bathing suits. Hers was missing.

"I have an idea where she might have gone," Wil said while tugging his jeans on. "I'm running down to the pool. You stay here in case I miss her on my way."

He pulled a fresh T-shirt over his head then ran out of the room, down the stairs, through the lobby, and out the back to where the pool was. He saw that the gate was open and heard splashing. For some reason, though, he didn't feel a sense of relief. Something didn't feel right.

He rushed over to the gate and saw two other children playing in the kiddie pool with a woman sitting in a folding chair beside it. He scanned the rest of the pool area. No Dakota.

"Excuse me," he said to the woman. "Was there a little girl in here while you've been here? About nine, this tall, long strawberry blonde hair? She would have been wearing a bathing suit with palm trees all over it."

The woman slid her sunglasses down her nose and peered up at him over the rims. "Um… yeah. I think we saw a little girl that looked like that leaving just as we came in."

Wil's heart pounded so hard in his chest he put his hand over his ribcage to slow it down. "Was she alone?"

"No. There was some man with her. Dark hair, tall, muscular, goatee, and dressed very nice. He seemed like he was in a real rush. The girl didn't look very happy to see him, but she went with him. It seemed like she knew who he was. I just assumed she was in trouble for coming down here without supervision."

From the woman's description, it didn't sound like Uncle Frank. He was more on the short and stocky side. Suddenly, Wil felt his body explode into a cold sweat. He thanked the woman then ran back to the room faster than he'd thought humanly possible.

He flung the door open to see Gramps jamming their stuff back into their duffle bags. Gramps jumped at the sound of the door handle hitting the wall.

"She's gone. I think one of Frank's guys took her."

Gramps took a deep breath then released it slowly. "Wasn't one of Frank's guys that got her."

"How do you—"

"Get in there and have the fastest shower you can have and still get clean. Trust me, you need it. I'm gonna get us packed up and checked out."

"What's wrong with you? I can't take a shower now. We've gotta get—"

"Just do what I tell ya, boy. I'll meet you in the car in exactly five minutes. Not one second longer or I'll leave without ya."

"Leave for where? What's going on, Gramps?"

"Saw the SUV driving out of the parking lot just as you ran out. It wasn't one of Frank's boys that took Dakota. It was Antonio. And I know where he took her."

Chapter Eight

Wil took the fastest shower known to man and then met Gramps down in the truck, who was already buckled in and had the engine running.

"We gotta go west to Qu'appelle Road until we hit Broadview Airport," he said while Wil strapped his seatbelt. "Antonio has a small bungalow just off the road and has a private plane he stores in a hanger by the airstrip."

"At some point you're going to share with me how you know all of this crap, right? I'm getting tired of asking."

"I'm getting just as tired of you asking me."

"You know what, you old coot? If it weren't for the fact that some little girl is out there with some freakazoid who's trying to take her to Caesar knows where, I'd slam this vehicle into park until you told me the whole story. I'm tired of all the cloak and dagger stuff."

"Well, look at that. I think my grandson actually does care about someone else besides himself. Holy Hannah, let's mark down the date and time."

Wil shook his head. "Nice. Really. Just like you to throw a sarcastic remark out there in order to avoid the question."

"Your job is to keep those baby blues on the road ahead. The turnoff won't be too much longer."

The two stayed silent for several minutes. Gramps stared out the windshield, his hands in tight fists on his knees. Wil reached over and switched the radio on, but there was no reception. The only thing that came through was the CBC radio broadcast of a soap opera. Gramps switched it back off.

"Saints alive. I'd rather listen to the tires on the road than that super fluff."

"I forgot what day it was." Wil glanced over to see Gramps frowning at him. "You know... the soaps are only on during the week? Lost track of the days already, I guess. Forget it. I ramble when I'm stressed."

Gramps reached over and gripped Wil's thigh. "Just drive, son. Things will work themselves out soon."

Wil gnawed at a hangnail on his thumb. At that point, he wasn't sure what caused him more anxiety: facing Antonio, worrying that Dakota was safe, or the fact that his grandfather was so calm.

Sure, Gramps never got rattled very easily. Essentially, he'd watched and experienced stuff in history people Wil's age only read about in school. Gramps had been born in 1915 in severe poverty somewhere in Europe. He knew people who'd died on the Titanic. He'd grown up in the Great Depression and even served in the military in two wars. He'd seen times go from telegraphs to cell phones, silent movies to 3D, radio to digital TV. How cool, but weird, all of that must have been.

Wil didn't know the intimate details in any of those situations because Gramps was pretty tight-lipped about his past and who he'd met in it. But Wil saw the emotions rise in his grandfather's eyes whenever he touched on anything from his past. It was a glimmer of memories, not just information he came across. And that was exactly what Wil's gut had screamed at him since Dakota came into their lives.

Gramps didn't just know something. He was close to the

situation, somehow. Wil read it all over his grandfather's face. Even though he didn't know everything there was to know about him, there was no way his grandfather would get that involved in a stranger's life. He'd have found a way to help the girl, sure. But Gramps wouldn't risk his life, or Wil's, for someone he'd just met.

Would he?

Ugh. Maybe Wil didn't know a thing. He thought he understood himself and where he was going, but Gramps had made him feel otherwise. Before the stupid road trip, he'd had everything planned and figured out. Now he was questioning all of his life's decisions, thinking about his parents, and allowing his grandfather to drag him on some blind search-and-rescue mission.

Wil's attention snapped back to his role of getaway driver when Gramps shouted orders at him to turn off.

"Turn left on that road up there. It goes all the way up to the Broadview Airport."

"By 'road' do you mean that stretch of dirt with the tire tracks in it?"

"That's how roads looked back when I was your age."

"Back when you drove your dinosaur-pulled cart?"

"Hilarious. Just—"

"Shut up and drive. Yeah, yeah. But the road disappears into the trees, and the area is surrounded by a fence. Are we allowed to go down there?"

Gramps shrugged. "Wasn't private property the last time I was out this way. And there's no sign. Besides, can't tell people to stay out when you aren't doing right. Right?"

"Well, I don't know. If they have snipers hiding around there, that would be enough to keep me out."

"There's not. Not anymore."

Wil flicked Gramps a side glare. "Really? Is that the best you can do? You'll excuse me if I don't find that very comforting."

Gramps turned his body to face Wil as best as he could still being strapped into his seatbelt. "Listen, boy. If I thought the worst would happen, I'da come out here on my own and left you back at the hotel. Get this fancy truck going or we'll miss our chance to get that girl back forever."

Wil shook his head then slipped the truck back into drive and turned off onto the mud road. The road wasn't meant for small cars, so he was glad to be in a solid truck rather than his half-dead hatchback. There was no cement or gravel. Just a stretch of thick, dried mud with deep tire tracks from the last time it had rained.

The tires bounced over the small bumps and sank into the deep grooves. The two men flailed around in their seats like popcorn starting to go in hot oil. Gramps held onto the dashboard with one hand and the door handle with the other while Wil simply tolerated his head slamming into the ceiling and his window frame. He was afraid if he took one of his hands off the steering wheel, he'd lose control of the truck.

Note to self, he thought. *Bring a helmet from this point on whenever traveling with Gramps.*

Finally, after what felt like hours, the road seemed to smooth out. Wil eased, rubbed the top of his head, and pushed down on the gas. He squinted into the distance and saw a clearing a few kilometers ahead of them. He sped up a bit more, hoping there was no hidden radar cop car in the brush, clocking drivers.

As they got through the clearing, Wil gasped. The area had been gutted out into a massive circular shape with two landing strips in the middle. At the opposite end from where they were, he saw a small hangar with a smaller building beside it. And there was the red SUV parked right in front.

He switched his focus to the small plane set up on one of the landing spots and an icy explosion filled his throat. A man he guessed was Antonio, by the description from the lady back at the pool, pulled Dakota by her forearms from the small building into the direction of the plane.

"Gun it, boy!" Gramps yelled. "Your daddy built this baby for speed. Let's see what she's got."

With a trigger response, Wil floored the gas, pushing the truck as fast as it could go. The faster they got, the louder the engine roared. His dad would have been proud. It wasn't exactly a vehicle one would use for a military stealth mission, but it didn't matter at that point.

As they got closer, Wil noticed that Antonio looked in their direction and paused. Then he put both of Dakota's wrists in one hand, reached behind him and pulled out what Wil assumed to be a gun.

Oh, no.

The truck cab vibrated from going a speed it hadn't been at for years, and the two men leaned forward in their seats. Dakota started kicking and screaming, so Antonio picked her up and flung her over his shoulder.

"C'mon, boy. Just a little bit further. If he gets on the plane..."

"I'm going as fast as I can!"

Antonio wasn't much bigger than Wil, so he seemed to be having trouble keeping steady as Dakota continued kicking.

Good for you, girl. Keep fighting.

Antonio managed to get the little girl only a few precious feet away from the plane. Suddenly, Dakota slammed her foot right into Antonio's gut, causing him to stumble forward, and they both tumbled to the ground. It was just enough of a delay to give Wil and Gramps a chance to close in. Wil slammed on the brakes, fumbled with his seat belt, then flung his door open.

Gramps was already running out of the car. "It's over, Antonio! Let her go."

Dakota scrambled to get up to her feet, but Antonio grabbed her and pulled her tightly to his chest. He whipped out a pistol that looked like something one of Adolf Hitler's men would have used. Wil knew nothing about guns, and didn't want to, but it looked similar to ones he'd seen in pictures from Gramps' old army days.

"You don't wanna do this, son."

"I have no idea how you found us here, but this is as far as you're going. My brother called to say you... took care of my kid. I appreciate that. But she's with me now."

Wil stepped forward. "You aren't taking her anywhere."

"Who's gonna stop me? You?"

Antonio held the pistol out in front of Dakota's face, aiming at the two men. Wil held his hands up and stepped back again.

"Yeah, I didn't think so. This is how this is going to happen. Me and my daughter are going to get on that plane, and we're going to go somewhere no one will find us. And you aren't going to follow us, right?"

"That's no way to raise a kid, son," Gramps said. "They'll be looking for you, and they won't give up until they find you. You know that. Do you really want your daughter to live that way? On the run?"

"What are you, a shrink? She'll be fine. She's with me. I won't let anything happen to her."

"You've already let things happen to her," Wil interjected. "You left her to be cared for by a couple who never gave a crap about her beyond the money they got for taking care of her. None of the money you gave them went to her. They used it for themselves."

Antonio stared at Wil, his black eyes burning into Wil's. "Yeah. I figured that. I took care of Frank and that fat, stupid, useless woman who leeched onto him. He called me, I got my people to find out what was really going on, then I sprang."

The icy wave in Wil's throat turned burning hot and slid down into his gut. *Did he just say he killed his own brother?*

"Frank was useless anyway." Antonio waved the gun at Wil. "Anyway, who cares? I appreciate you watching out for my girl, but I got things covered from here."

Gramps glared. "We'll go, but we're taking little Dakota here with us. She needs her mama and I made a promise to get her back to her."

Antonio's face flushed. His eyes narrowed. "Just who do you think you are, old man? This is *my* kid. I can take care of her the way she needs to be taken care of."

"No you can't, son. Money isn't all you need to take care of a child. She needs a mother's love. She's not a possession, like your cars or that plane. She's a child, and no child deserves to live on the run."

"You know what? This conversation is over. You aren't my father, my parole officer, or my therapist." He held the pistol right up in Gramps' face. "You're just some stupid, old jerk with a grandson whose McGuffys are big enough to stand up to my greasy-haired brother for a little girl. Bravo. Thank you. Now get outta my way or I'll have to off you right in front of the kid."

Gramps stood his ground. He didn't flinch.

"What's wrong with you? I just got rid of my own flesh and blood. You don't think I'd have an issue offing some stupid old goat or a young punk I don't even know?"

Not one muscle moved.

"I'm giving you the chance to walk away here. I don't do that."

Gramps inched up closer toward Antonio. Wil tried grabbing him back, but he held up his hand. Then he said, "I don't think you'll do something else that would make your granddaddy disappointed in you."

Wil's eyes widened. He noticed that the end of the gun started shaking.

"What do you know about my granddaddy?" Antonio's voice quivered.

Gramps lifted his head to meet Antonio's glare. "I know that he was a good man who started a business that his son and grandsons turned dirty. I know that he loved his family more than his own life and spent his days protecting, covering for, and paying off their dirty deeds. And I know that he wanted to keep one part of his family pure and untarnished by keeping her away from all that could harm her."

Antonio's hand shook the gun so much Wil feared he'd squeeze the trigger by accident. He was ready to jump in front of Gramps.

"Who are you, old man?"

Gramps walked right up to the gun so the shaft pressed into his chest. "Your granddaddy tell you about a man he called Iron Guts?"

Antonio tilted his head and squinted. He let his arm fall back down to his side but kept his grip on Dakota. "Well, yeah. The guy saved Granddaddy's life in Korea. Something about getting surprised with bombs and snipers. Everyone else got killed. That Iron Guts, with shrapnel in his legs, carried Granddaddy all the way to some abandoned shack and took care of him until they were found by one of those M.A.S.H. units. Without that guy, our family wouldn't have happened. It was a story he yapped about every time the family got together for holidays and the wine was going around."

Gramps nodded. "He tell you anything else?"

"I don't know, maybe something else the guy did when I was a kid." Antonio released a sharp breath then snapped the gun back up in Gramps' face. "This conversation is all very interesting, but as you can see, I got a plane to catch here. So if you got something else you wanna say—"

"You were about eight when you got sick, is that right?"

The color drained from Antonio's face. He flicked a look at Wil then shifted his eyes back at Gramps. Wil's heart pounded in his ears.

"How do you—?"

"You had leukemia and needed a bone marrow donor. No one in your family was a match, so they had to look outside. You were pretty close to death when your granddaddy contacted me. See, he remembered my blood type when we served together and knew I was a pretty healthy guy."

Wil put his hand over his mouth. He remembered hearing a story one of his aunts had told him once of how Gramps had saved a young boy's life. She'd never given him all of the details. Wil just assumed he'd stopped a car from hitting the kid or saved him from drowning or something.

Gramps went on. "Guess they matched us up and sucked stuff out of my spine so you could be strong enough to fight that nasty cancer. Musta worked, because here you are."

Tears flooded Wil's eyes. Antonio's chin quivered as Gramps continued, but he held his stance.

"I guess you could say that, technically, you got some of Iron Guts's blood flowing through your veins. Which means it's in hers, too. So if you think for one minute I'm going to let you destroy this precious jewel's life the way you've done your own, you got another think coming."

"Why did you do it?" Antonio's voice trembled.

"What? Give the marrow? Because your granddaddy was one of the greatest men I knew. He's helped our family too. That's what folks are supposed to do." Gramps reached out for the gun. "And because you meant the world to him. Couldn't just let a young one die when I had a way to help make things right."

Wil hugged himself. His eyes darted from one man to the other. Suddenly, he was distracted by a high-pitched scream in the distance.

Police sirens?

Antonio eased his grip on Dakota and she ran to Wil, power-hugging him. Antonio shifted his gaze past Gramps to the six RCMP vehicles and paddy wagon speeding toward them.

"You aren't a killer, son!" Gramps yelled over the nearing

sirens. "You went down a bad path and got so far down you couldn't get out. But you aren't this kind of bad. That girl belongs with her mama, and you gotta do right by her." Then he pointed up. "And your granddaddy."

The cops got closer. The two men stared each other down, then Antonio reached out and grabbed Gramps' forearm. Wil was ready to shove Dakota to the ground and pounce until he saw the greasy gangster shoved the handle of the gun into Gramps' palm. "I'd rather give this up to you than those guys." He kept the old man's hand between his own.

"You saved our family doing what you did for Granddaddy. I might seem like a real jerk, but he was my hero. It was Dad who decided to take on more of the... questionable businesses. Then that moron brother of mine picked up the ball and took it right to illegal. I tried stopping it all, but couldn't. So I just covered up everything and, well, got sent down the toilet."

Wil shook his head. It was like watching a movie that he couldn't turn off. The RCMP cars were close enough to them now and all skidded to a stop. Amid the dust their cars kicked up, the officers got out of their cars and held guns up in their direction.

"Antonio Rossi!" One of the officers shouted. "Stand down and surrender your weapon! If you give up now, the only additional charges will be failing to report to your parole officer and disobeying the order to stay away from the girl."

Antonio seemed to ignore the officer and spoke with more urgency to Gramps. "I never wanted things to go the way they did. After a while it was hard to stop it all from snowballing. By the time I found out about the clubs, the drugs, and the dirty money in the books, it was too late. And my name was on everything."

"...and you set up that policy for the girl."

"No. Granddaddy set up the policy for her, as well as the trust funds, with the twist that she'd get the money if something happened to me. His way of making sure I didn't go too far over the edge, you know what I mean? And he's the one that set that fund up for you, too."

Fund? Wil thought. Was that where Gramps' money came from? Wil had thought it was from his military and employment retirement.

"Now that's a little different from what I heard, but it makes perfect sense. And we owe him our thanks for all he did after this one's parents were killed. Sure helped. Never got a chance to thank him."

Wil swallowed past the lump in his throat. It all made sense. His grandfather gave huge yearly donations to MADD and to brain and spinal cord research. His parents had been killed by a drunk truck driver. His mother had died instantly when she was thrown through the windshield, but his father had stayed in a coma for weeks with brain and spine injuries. Gramps must have been giving the money Antonio's granddaddy had sent him to those charities. He wondered if the man had paid for his dad's hospital bills too.

"I think you just did." Antonio knelt down and laced his fingers together behind his head. "Let's do this."

Gramps nodded then held Antonio's pistol up over his head. "He surrendered his weapon. Come take him, boys."

Four of the RCMP officers ran over to them, two going to arrest Antonio while the other two approached Wil, Gramps, and Dakota to see if they were injured and to take their statements.

After fifteen minutes, Gramps and Wil were told they were free to go while Antonio was taken over to a squad car. An older officer, who must have been a Chief of Police of some kind, walked up and gripped Gramps' hand.

"Wilf, gotta thank you for all your help back there. Without your quick thinking, we might have missed him."

Gramps waved the officer off with a sputter. "Wasn't anything. Just doing my civic duty, is all."

"Oh, it's a lot more than that and you know it. And we appreciate it." Then the officer turned to Dakota. "Well, now, sweet one. How would you feel about seeing your mama?"

Dakota's eyes got wider than Wil thought humanly possible. "Really?" she asked. "Oh my *goodness*. I would *so* love that. But am I allowed to?"

"All is good now. But you'll have to let me and my friend, Officer Saunders over there, take you. Wil and his grandfather have been awesome in helping out, but they won't be able to take you home. That's our job."

The young girl dipped her chin down. "Can I say goodbye?"

"Of course. Take all the time you need."

Dakota turned to Gramps and wrapped her arms around his torso. "I am so happy I met you. You aren't nearly as grouchy as Wil says. I think you're funny. And I'll always think of you whenever I hug Lamby Junior."

Gramps moved his arms around the girl, hugging her back. "You are a little sweetheart. I'm glad we met too. And speaking of Lamby, don't forget this." He pulled the stuffie out of his pocket and handed it to her.

She clutched it to her chest, then she faced Wil and squeezed him. "I think I will miss you lots. I liked having a sort of big brother. And I will never forget how you stood up to my uncle. Thank you."

Wil's eyes stung with tears as he hugged Dakota as hard as she hugged him. Then she broke away, walking backwards to the officer. "Thank you. For everything. I will never forget you."

Before walking away, the officer said, "Well, Mr. Carter gave me his mailing address so you can write to them anytime you want to. You can keep them posted on how you're doing."

"Oh, I will. I promise!"

With that, the officer shook both men's hands, thanked Gramps again, then escorted Dakota to the waiting unmarked squad car. The two men watched the car disappear through the trees then started making their way back over to the truck. Suddenly, Antonio's voice made Gramps stop in his tracks.

"Hey! Iron Guts! I didn't kill my brother. I just sent him off. You know... just so you know..."

Gramps' lips stretched into a small smile. All he did was hold his hand up then kept walking. Wil walked behind his grandfather at a much slower pace, staring at the back of the man's head as they inched back to the car. He'd learned more about Gramps in that hour than he had his entire life. The man was a hero in every sense of the word. Why would he not want others to know those wonderful things he'd done? It had to do with a lot more than modesty. And he had a feeling their mob experience was only the tip of the iceberg.

Gramps got into the passenger's seat but left the door open. Wil decided to do a quick walk around the truck to assess any damage. The body had a few dents from the race across the dirt road and it was in desperate need of a wash, but everything seemed okay.

He climbed in the driver's seat and adjusted his body behind the wheel. The two men sat there for a few minutes, looking out the windshield. A helicopter flew overhead. A warm, dry breeze blew through the cab. Then Wil slammed his door shut and turned the engine over. Gramps shut his door then strapped his seatbelt on.

Wil looked in the rearview mirror at the empty back seat. Then he felt a pat on his knee.

"I'm going to miss her too, boy."

"Do you think she's going to be okay?"

"From this point on."

"How did the officers know where to find us?"

"Called 'em on your cell while you were in the shower and gave them the coordinates on the GPS doamahickey you showed me how to use."

Wil faced his grandfather and frowned. "Say what now?"

"I don't think I stuttered."

"But you were cranking at me not to explain it all to you. You told me it was too spacey and technical."

"Guess I had my hearing aid on at the time and was payin' attention."

Wil put the truck into drive, did a U-turn, and drove back toward the dirt road leading out of the field. They made their way through the trees then back up to the highway. He got up to the turn off and back onto the Trans-Canada and stopped.

"What are you waiting for? Christmas ain't for another five months."

"Why didn't you tell me any of that stuff about you? You know… the money, the Rossis, saving lives…?"

Gramps shrugged, keeping his eyes straight ahead. "Ain't stuff that comes up in everyday conversation. No big deal."

"No big deal? Are you kidding me? You're, like, this superhero dude. You have definitely shot up in the respect scale a few thousand notches."

"Well, thanks so much, son. You make it sound like there wasn't much to begin with. Not that you've ever hidden that well."

"Well, what can I say? It's hard to respect a guy who can fart to the tune of 'Mac the Knife.'"

"Think of the stories you'll have to tell your friends or children one day."

"My friends have had a front row seat to that special talent, thanks so much."

"I'm old. These things can just happen. Out of my control. One day, you'll have the joy of feeling what age does to a man's body."

"Wonderful."

Wil pulled back onto the Trans-Canada. They drove a short stretch, then Wil said, "Seriously, though. You saved another life today. You're awesome."

"Don't know about that, but you had a hand in it."

"Not really."

"Wouldn't have happened if you'd kept your little girl panties on."

Wil choked down the urge to give sarcastic retort. "You are one super cool dude."

"Nice that I've gone from 'cranky old fart' to 'super cool dude'."

"You're still a cranky old fart. You broke the mold for that title."

"I'm proud of you too, son. It took guts to go into a situation like that blind. Thanks for trusting me."

"Guess I get it from you, Iron Guts."

Wil flicked Gramps a look and saw he was repressing a smile.

There was nothing but open road ahead of them. And the rest of Gramps' secrets.

For some reason, Wil didn't feel quite as uneasy about what was to come.

Please just no more gangsters, runaway kids, or guns, he thought. *I'm not sure my sanity can take much more.*

Chapter Nine

After traveling for another half-hour, Wil finally broke the silence. "So, uh, you gonna tell me where to next? Or is it useless to even ask?"

"Heading for Indian Head."

Wil frowned. "Is that a town or a landmark?"

"Well, let's see. You asked me where we're going to next, and I said 'Indian Head.' Safe bet that I meant a town."

"Can you, maybe, for once answer a question without the witty sarcasm?"

"Only if you can ask a question that doesn't have an obvious answer."

"Okay, just forget it." Wil waved his hand at Gramps. "So, what's in Indian Head?"

"A couple of things. We'll stay there overnight at this bed and breakfast I know, then we'll go on to White City. That'll be our final destination."

Wil smiled. It wasn't just a plan, it was like a military op or something. And the old man was determined to see it out to the end. Wil had to give him credit. He just hoped whatever was supposed to happen next would be more on the tamer side of things.

"Before we head down that way, though, we have to stop off in Grenfell. Got someone there I have to talk to."

"Of course," said Wil with a snort. "The last time you said that, we got into some trouble."

"Yeah, well… I can guarantee you nothing like that will happen again on this trip."

"Guarantee me, huh?"

"Yup."

"You'll excuse me if I don't totally believe you."

The two men remained silent until they drove past the sign for Grenfell. Gramps broke the silence. "All right, we don't actually have to go too far. The church is just in town."

"Another church?"

"You survived the first time, didn't ya?"

"Barely."

"Oh just shut up and drive down that street there. You can't miss it."

Wil slowed the speed and drove down the street until he saw a large blue building. *Well, he's right,* thought Wil. *You certainly can't miss it.*

Unlike the first church, Trinity Presbyterian was much bigger and a bit more modern. Wil pulled up into the parking lot and Gramps clambered out. He started worrying that his grandfather wasn't getting the rest he needed. With all the excitement from the last few days, Gramps seemed a bit slower… a little paler.

"Gramps? You wanna take a rest first? You didn't sleep in the car and, well, with all that Frank-Antonio stuff…"

"I'm fine, boy. Stop fussing over me. I'll rest later."

Wil drew in a breath and shook his head. There was no point in even trying to force him to slow down. He just had a gut feeling that something was wrong. Something had triggered all of his grandfather's sudden need to show Wil his past. The young man shrugged it off then followed Gramps to the front door of the church.

The building was much more open than the older one they'd visited earlier on. Wil figured they had a larger congregation, judging by the number of pews. And they must have had a strong musical focus as there was a nicer organ and choir loft.

Gramps made his way up to the front of the church then called out, "Reverend Fulton? Are you around?" His voice echoed around the room.

A man, maybe in his fifties or so, came out from a door next to the choir loft. "Wilf? Is that you?"

He approached Gramps with his hands held out. Gramps held one hand out while gripping one of the pews with the other for stability. Wil frowned.

"Oh, are you all right? You seem a bit unsteady there."

The old man grunted. "Just my blasted hip. Old war injury. Comes and goes, you know. Too much walking without resting enough, I guess."

"Let's sit here, then." The reverend motioned to a pew. "Sitting in the car isn't exactly resting that hip, now, is it?"

"Guess not. And we've had a bit more excitement the last few days than I'm used to."

That's the understatement of the year, Wil thought.

The reverend laughed. "Yes, well, knowing you, I'm sure you tackled it all like an angry bear. Excitement seems to follow you, from what I remember."

Gramps released a snicker. After a few minutes of small talk about the weather and the road trip, he pointed at Wil with his thumb. "This here is my grandson, Wil. Wil, this is Reverend Fulton. His dad worked for me many years ago."

Wil stuck his hand out to the reverend then nodded. "Nice to meet you, sir."

"Oh, please. This is all too formal. Please call me Dave. And it's wonderful to finally put a face to the name. Your grandfather is very proud of you."

Wil repressed an eye roll and thought, *It'd be nice to hear it from the source once in a while.*

"How are things going around here? Building up a following?" Gramps shifted his position on the hard bench.

"We're doing very well. Thanks to your help, we've been able to rebuild and repair a few areas. We've even started that community garden out back, as you suggested. We are very grateful to you."

Wil's frown must have caught Dave's attention because he smiled and directed the conversation his way. "Your grandfather is one of our most loyal and generous donors. He's not only helped build this place of worship from the ground up, he's also helped us maintain it and give back to the community. We have several families around here in high need. He gives us ways to help them by getting them to help themselves."

Gramps shrugged. "Bah! It isn't anything any other man wouldn't do. Giving skills or teaching a trade is better than just handing over a bunch of money. Money disappears pretty fast. The skill or trade can be reused."

Wil remembered hearing the exact same expression when Gramps told him to get a job. His grandfather never just handed money over to Wil. He had to work for everything, no matter how small the sum. He'd thought Gramps was the biggest hard-butt in the world. Right then, he finally got what Gramps had been trying to teach him back then.

"Well, you did the same thing for my dad. Giving him a job so he could take care of all of us instead of just handing him a loan, like he originally asked for, made a difference."

"Well, sakes alive, son. There were seven of you kids plus your mom. And since he wasn't from here, he didn't have many job options. He ended up being one of my best workers. He was a good man."

The reverend bowed his head, putting his hand on Gramps' knee. "He was. Last of a dying breed, for sure. And we miss him every day."

Wil's gaze shifted back and forth between the two men. "What happened to him, if you don't mind my asking?"

The two men looked at him. "I don't mind, Wil. My father was killed by a drunk driver several years ago now. Your grandfather has been an even stronger support system for my family since then. Go see the plaque up front."

Gramps suddenly seemed uncomfortable. Wil walked up to the front of the church. There on the front of the pulpit was a picture of Gramps with who he assumed to be Reverend Fulton's father. It had obviously been taken many years earlier, since the photo was in black and white and Gramps was much younger. The two men were surrounded by seven children. The plaque read: "In loving memory of Andrew Fulton. A good man, a model father, a kindred spirit. Your life will always be celebrated here. Wilf Carter."

Wil turned around and gaped at his grandfather. Gramps, of course, avoided his eyes. He started seeing the old man in a totally different way. And it was... pretty cool.

After a brief but uncomfortable silence, Gramps cleared his throat. "Okay, well. We'd best be going. Got a bit more driving to do before we can have a rest. Just wanted to stop by and see how things are going."

Dave patted Gramps' knee once more then helped him stand up. "We are doing marvelously, thanks to you. Here. I'll walk you out."

The three men walked to the door, then the reverend let go of Gramps' arm and opened the door for him and Wil. "Thanks for stopping by. You'll have to come back at harvest time and see what the garden gives us."

A shadow of sadness passed over Gramps' face. "I'd sure like that. Can't say for sure we'll be back out this way then. But you know I'll stop in if we are."

"Anytime, Wilf. And it was very nice to meet you, Wil. Take care of this man. The world needs him here."

Wil nodded then followed Gramps to the truck. They got in and buckled up without saying a word. Wil started up the engine and gave Gramps a peek from the corner of his eye. He noticed tears pooled in the old man's lower lids.

"You okay?"

Gramps gave a sharp nod and wiped his eyes. "Yep. Fine. Those are some good people, son. Always giving to and helping others, even when they had very little or nothing."

"Well from what it sounds like, you've been doing the exact same thing."

"That's what life is all about, son. Giving to others when it's needed. It all comes back to ya in some way. Good or bad. You put good out there, good comes back."

"See? You're going all Confucius on me again. It makes me nervous."

Gramps smacked the dashboard with his palm. "This ain't a joke, son. I really thought this would teach you that some stuff in life is more than jokes and pokes. You gotta pull that head outta your butt and start taking things more seriously. I won't be here forever and you just *gotta* take better care."

Wil swallowed. Gramps rarely yelled at him. Sure he squawked a lot, but he never raised his voice. His view was that when you yell, a person tunes you out a lot more than when you speak calmly. Gramps' sudden burst of anger churned his insides with guilt.

"I'm sorry, Gramps. I was just kidding. I guess you're right. Maybe I do joke too much. But that's what we do. I jab you, you jab me... I was just trying to lighten the mood."

"I know." Gramps sighed. "Didn't mean to yell. Guess a lot has gone on, and I need more shut-eye than I thought. Let's get us over to Indian Head and find that bed and breakfast I told you about earlier. Should only be another half-hour or so. We'll have some grub, hit the hay early, then we can head out to White City in the morning."

Wil pulled out of the church parking lot and back out

onto the highway without another word. As he drove, the twinge of worry that gnawed at him earlier grew. It wasn't just the past days events that were making Gramps so tired and emotional. Each stop they'd made and each person they'd met on their little trip gave Wil a tiny bit more into his grandfather's past. It almost felt like the more his grandfather revealed of himself, the more vulnerable he became... weaker. He shook his head and noticed the sign welcoming them to the "Town of Indian Head."

Hopefully, things will slow down a bit so Gramps can.

****

Following Gramps' not-so-accurate directions, they finally pulled up in front of the Cornerhouse Bed and Breakfast just before seven o'clock. Wil was exhausted, starving, and in desperate need of a shower, so he only imagined how his grandfather must have been feeling.

He noticed, though, that Gramps seemed to brighten a bit the moment they drove into the small town. It was as if some new life was breathed into him. Or a familiarity flashed across his face. Wil couldn't be certain. He thought he'd known his grandfather pretty well until the last few days. All he knew was that it was nice to see a smile on the old man's usually stern face.

Maybe it's just gas, he thought.

"Alrighty, we're here." Wil undid his seatbelt and grabbed his cell phone from the seat between them. "How do we check in to such a place? I've never stayed in a bed and breakfast."

Gramps already had his seatbelt off and was opening his door. "Not the same as a hotel. This is more like staying in someone's house. Don't embarrass yourself."

"And how would I do that?"

"All ya gotta do most days is open that mouth of yours.

The rest happens naturally."

"Well, thanks a lot for the confidence. You make me sound like a Neanderthal or something."

Gramps swung himself out of the vehicle then slammed his door. "Wouldn't give you that much credit," he said as he shuffled to the front steps of the house. "Cavemen have better social skills."

Wil walked around the front of the truck repressing a giggle. "Nice. Very nice. Well, if my social skills are less than satisfactory, maybe you should be asking yourself where I learned them."

Gramps waved Wil off and mumbled something inaudible as he pulled himself up the front stairs. Wil noticed he was moving a bit better than he had back at the church. For some reason, that gave him a huge sense of relief.

"I'll be on my very best behavior. I promise," Wil said. "And by the way? I find it fascinating that you have no idea who Confucius is, but you're so familiar with Neanderthals."

The old man stopped at the top of the stairs then turned to face Wil, peering at him over the top of his glasses. "I learned about cavemen, son. We can learn a lot about ourselves from them. Can't say the same thing about some young fella who speaks all fancy about what he *thinks* life is all about. I'd trust what a caveman had to tell me a lot more."

Wil stitched his eyebrows. He couldn't tell if Gramps was making a joke or giving him crap again so he decided to keep his mouth closed. Gramps opened the front door to the house, holding it open for Wil, then stepped inside.

The house was three stories with a huge veranda wrapped around the front and side, leading into an enormous backyard. Wil wasn't sure how many bedrooms the place had, but it reminded him of one of those smaller southern mansions he'd seen in movies. As the door shut behind them, Wil stifled a gasp at the beauty of the inside.

The floors were shiny dark wood — cherry? Mahogany?

He couldn't tell for sure. The staircase leading to the upper floors reminded Wil of the infamous stairs in "Gone With the Wind." In fact, the entire place reminded him of one of those fancy houses with all of the dramatic drapes and lacy window coverings. He noticed, though, that there were sprinkles of modern times amid all the beautiful, old-fashioned furniture: the biggest flat-screen TV he'd ever seen hung on the wall in the living room, and three computers were set up in the corner of the room on different work desks.

Gramps' voice brought him out of his daze. "Close your mouth, son. You look like a hound watching someone eat a steak."

Wil chose not to give a retort. "Where is everyone? Are you sure that there'll be a room for us?"

A smile tugged up one side of Gramps' lips. "I'm pretty sure we'll get a room."

Just as Wil was about to ask how he knew, a voice shouted from the direction of the kitchen. "Sorry for the delay, folks. Heard you come in. Go on into the living room and get comfortable. I'll be right out."

They left their bags by the door then moved toward the main room, the floorboards creaking and groaning with each step. Wil sat on the faux leather loveseat and Gramps plopped down into the plush armchair set closest to the fireplace. He must have misjudged the softness of the chair and sank right into it, the cushion hugging around him so much his feet stuck straight out like a five-year old child's.

"Help! The flippin' thing is eating me!"

Wil laughed so hard he couldn't lift himself up to help his grandfather. Instead he fell over on his side, holding his stomach. "Holy Hannah, Gramps. You look like a couch sandwich."

"Glad I can entertain you, boy. Can you manage to pull yourself together long enough to get me out of here? I'm losing sensation in my legs."

That made Wil laugh even harder, and tears streamed down his cheeks. Right then, a slight, older woman with fire-engine-red hair and the greenest eyes Wil had ever seen appeared beside the chair.

"Well, bless my soul. If it isn't Wilf Carter. You always seem to manage to get yourself into these messes, don't ya now?"

Gramps grimaced. "Well, since my grandson is too busy laughing his butt off over there, would you be so kind as to help an old man out of an embarrassing situation?"

The woman laughed and held out her hands. Gramps took hold of them, then with one smooth yank, he was pulled out of the chair's grip. The two held hands for a few more seconds until Gramps cleared his throat. "Son, this here is an old family friend. I want you to say 'How do you do?' to Anya Flannery. Anya, this here is my grandson, Wil."

She dropped Gramps' hands, holding hers out to Wil. "Well just look at ya. You are the spitting image of your granddad here at the same age, sure as I'm standing here. Oh, I knew him back then." She leaned closer to Wil, whispering loud enough for Gramps to hear. "Had the biggest crush on him, I hafta admit."

Wil smiled, noticing his grandfather's cheeks tinged red. "Well, I can totally understand that. He's quite a catch."

"All right, you. Keep it shut. Uh, Anya? My grandson and I were wondering if you had that room up on the top floor available for a night."

Anya let go of one of Wil's hands, held the other between her palms, then said, "Well, you know that room is always free for you. Will ya be in town long?"

"No. Just thought I'd take the boy on a bit of a road trip to teach him a few important things about life."

"Ah. Same trip you made with your son years back?" She patted Wil's hand then let it go. "Did he ever get that truck finished?"

Gramps nodded. "Sure did. We drove it out."

"That's just wonderful. Well, then. I hope you plan on taking him over to the old place. It's still there."

"This time we are." Gramps lowered his eyes. "Whole point of the trip, actually."

Wil wrinkled his brow. "What place?"

Anya looked at the young man, one side of her mouth lifting up into a half-smile. Gramps' eyes never looked up from the floor. "You'll find out tomorrow, my boy."

No one said a word for several seconds. Wil shifted his weight from one foot to the other. Anya walked over to Gramps and rubbed his shoulder. "All will be just fine. Now, why don't you two get whatever belongings you have for the night and follow me? Then you can get settled while I fix us a snack. I've already cleaned up from supper, but I think I can rustle us up some coffee and pie."

Gramps looked up at her over his glasses. "Your world-famous Dutch apple pie?"

She released a belly laugh and slapped her thighs. "Oh dear. I'm not sure it's 'world famous' but it sure has made a lot of folks happy." She walked out of the living room and over to the stairs.

The two men picked up their bags they'd left by the door then followed Anya up the three flights of stairs to their room. Gramps seemed to have a little bit more jump in his step as he scaled the stairs with greater ease than Wil. When they finally got to the top, Wil saw there were two rooms, some sort of sitting room and a large bathroom.

Anya guided the men to the last room and opened the door for them. Wil almost gasped. Compared to the rest of the house, which was decorated quite femininely, the room had a real... masculine vibe. There were two double beds and pictures of cars, planes, and war heroes on the walls. All of the window coverings, bedspreads, and furniture were in more earthy, darker greens, blues, and beige. And the side table between the beds was made out of fancy old tires. Framed pictures on the table caught Wil's eye, and he walked over to it, dropping his bag on a dark blue recliner by the door.

"Well, I'll let you boys get settled. Come down in about ten minutes or so and everything should be ready and waiting for you."

"Thanks for everything. We'll be there."

Wil heard the door close as he plunked down on one of the beds and stared at the photos. They were pictures of Gramps and the rest of their family. He didn't recognize everyone in a few of them because they were those black-and-white photos where no one smiled. One made his jaw drop. He reached over and picked it up.

"Gramps? This is you and dad."

Gramps shuffled over and dropped down beside Wil. "Yep. That's us when I brought him out this way. Anya took the picture just before we left."

In the picture the two men stood beside each other, their arms around each other's shoulders, frozen laughter plastered on their faces. Tears stung Wil's eyes. Not only was it nice to see Gramps' real smile, his dad looked just like he remembered. Rugged, happy, strong...

He put his fist up to his lips, trying to stop the tears. "How does this woman know you so well? And our family?"

"Well. You heard her say we knew each other way back when. Her mom used to run this place a really long time ago. I used to stay here in between truck stops, when I'd go on business trips, and even brought your Gran here on our honeymoon. This is the room they always put me in. Set it up to be sorta like a home away from home."

He stared at the photo in Wil's hands. "Your dad loved it here. He used to come here too. Brought your mom here. They were coming back from here when they got into the accident." Gramps leaned over, grabbed another photo, and handed it to Wil. "Haven't been back here since."

The other picture was of his parents. His dad held his mom in a deep dancing dip pose, both of them with goofy expressions on their faces. Tears overflowed from his lower lids. He wiped them away with the back of his hand.

Gramps patted Wil's knee then used it to stand up. "C'mon. Anya doesn't like being kept waiting. We'll have some pie, clean up, and hit the sack. We got one more stop to make before heading back to Winnipeg."

Wil stared at the picture of his parents as he heard Gramps walking away. He was finally starting to understand the purpose of the entire trip. Of all the people they'd met, the experiences, even Gramps' harsh lessons. He was helping Wil make a connection to his parents and to him. It didn't feel as weird or scary as he thought it would.

"C'mon, boy. If I miss my pie and coffee, I'll make you regret it."

"All right, already. Keep your big boy diaper on, I'm coming."

He chewed the inside of his lip, put the picture back on the night stand — facing his bed — followed Gramps out of the room. The smell of coffee and pie flooded his nostrils the second they started back down the stairs. His stomach growled in response.

After an hour filled with more pie than either of them should have had before bed, good hazelnut-flavored coffee, and wonderful conversations with stories of Anya and Gramps' younger days, Wil and his grandfather headed up to bed.

Gramps got the shower first, while Wil lay on his bed waiting for his turn. He closed his eyes and before he knew it, he fell into the deepest, most restful sleep he'd had in a long time.

Chapter Ten

The smell of coffee and bacon tempted Wil from his sleep. He opened his eyes just wide enough to be able to see the alarm clock on the nightstand.

9:07 a.m.

He frowned. Gramps never let him sleep in past eight o'clock, and that was considered "sleeping in." The room was even still dim, despite the bright sunlight trying to break through the drapes. If they'd been at home, Gramps would have already pulled the shades up and dragged Wil's sheets off in an attempt to get him up.

Wil shifted his gaze to Gramps' bed and noticed it was already made. His duffle bag lay in the middle of the bed, unzipped, with a few of his toiletries around it. Wil guessed his grandfather had gotten up at his usual, crazy early time of five-thirty, had his shower, read the newspaper, drank his pot of coffee, and Anya was then feeding him breakfast.

He dragged himself out of bed and was about to go down for breakfast when realized that he'd slept in his clothes. That would not go off well. Gramps would expect him to, at the very least, smell sub-human. He opted for a quick shower and a change of clothes before running downstairs.

While getting ready, thoughts flooded his mind. He didn't remember his parents the way he used to, and it hurt. But oddly, in the last week, he'd felt closer to them and his grandfather than he'd ever thought possible. He started remembering bits of memories from when he'd been little. His parents' faces didn't seem quite as faded. And he understood himself a bit better, too. Of course, he'd never admit all of that to his grandfather. He'd never hear the end of it.

As he walked down the last flight of stairs, and heard Anya and Gramps' voices mixed with the music on the local easy listening radio station, butterflies exploded in his stomach. Gramps mentioned that they had one more stop to make on their trip before heading back to Winnipeg. With all that they'd gone through, what could there possibly be left to see? Or learn? Or know? He shook his head and pasted on a smile.

Can't worry about that now. If I've learned nothing else lately, it's that I have no choice over what happens. Gotta deal with what comes.

"Well, will you look what the cat coughed up?" Gramps cranked his head in Wil's direction.

Wil sat down in the padded chair beside his grandfather. "Don't you mean 'what the cat dragged in'?"

"Nah. You look more like something it coughed up."

"Why thanks. We should really hire you out for self-esteem seminars. You'd make a killing."

Anya released a throaty laugh while putting a plate in front of each man. "Here ya are, then. Enough with the banter and fill those stomachs up. That should keep ya goin' until your next stop."

No kidding, Wil thought. Each plate was loaded with bacon, sunny-side up eggs, fried potatoes, and toast, with a bowl of fruit salad on the side. He would have been just fine with the toast and fruit but dug in anyway. And it wasn't until he started eating that he realized how hungry he was.

"Would ya look at that? This boy usually grazes on bagels or cereal. Can't get him to eat like this at home to save my soul."

Wil swallowed a mouthful of potatoes. "If you cooked like this, I'd eat it."

"Bah! You wouldn't know good cooking if it bit you in the butt."

"This is good cooking, dude. And my butt is grateful." The young man stopped mid-forkful, heat radiating across his cheeks. "Oh, ma'am. I am so sorry. I forgot where I was for a second."

"Doncha worry about it, son." Anya rubbed his back. "I've had four boys of my own. Not much makes this old girl blush. And don't be forgettin' that I hung out with that sly one for a while too." She winked and then walked over to the counter to grab the coffee pot.

Gramps' cheeks tinged red. "Anyway. Best be eating up pretty quick, so we can get going. Let ya sleep a bit longer so you'd be well-rested."

"Yeah. I noticed that. You must be getting soft or something."

"Must be all the fresh air. Don't get used to it. Things are back to normal when we get home."

"I'd expect nothing less."

Anya sauntered back to the table. "You two. Just like when you came here with your boy, Wilf. Same banter. Same love being hidden behind the sarcasm. Does my heart good. More coffee, anyone?"

Gramps held up his cup for a refill. "That boy needed the same guidance as this one here. Only this one needs a stronger kick."

"Ah. But his dad turned out all right in the end, didn't he?"

Gramps nodded. "Guess so. He's had a harder start than

his dad did. I gotta make sure to push him a little harder so he doesn't use that as a reason to stop. A hard start in life gives you a reason to make sure you keep moving forward."

Wil shook his head at the offer of more coffee then put his fork down on his plate. "First of all? Hello? It's me right beside you. You know I hate when you have conversations about me when I'm sitting right here. And secondly? Confucius."

"And why are we bringing up that guy again?"

"Because you keep making these diamond-in-the-rough philosophical statements that are, frankly, quite impressive. I think you should teach others the fine lessons of life. You could call it... 'The World According To Gramps.' No! Wait! Better still... 'Grampsfucius Says...'"

Wil burst into laughter, and Anya giggled from the sink.

Gramps breathed out sharply and said, "See? This is what I've had to put up with. Listen, boy. I've been trying to teach you all this time. If it ain't getting through that thick skull of yours by now what I'm trying to do—"

"Oh now, Wilf." Anya put her hand on Gramps' forearm as she reached to take his plate. "Give the boy a bit of a break. He's part of you, and right from that boy of yours, so I know he's a smart one. Plus he's got the heart of his mother in him. I can see it. You just have to take him out to the house. It'll all come together out there."

Gramps patted Anya's hand. She winked, took Wil's plate, and carried both over to the sink. The two men sat at the table, slouching over their coffee mugs in silence. The radio played "In My Life" by the Beatles. Cutlery, plates, and other dishes clanked in the sink as Anya rinsed everything off before putting it all in the dishwasher.

Wil broke the silence. "Anya? What were my parents like? You know, when they came here."

Drying her hands on a dishtowel, Anya turned around and walked back to the table. She pulled up a chair on the opposite side of them, laid the towel on the table, and slowly lowered herself down. "I'm very happy you decided to ask me that, young man. I've been waiting for you to bring them up since you got here." She folded her arms on the table then leaned forward.

"Well they were about the most loving couple I'd seen around here in quite some time. Couldn't take their eyes away from each other for less than a minute or two, I'd say. Always teasing each other... laughing. Your dad, he was the joker... never seeming to take things too seriously. Your mom, now, she was the one to keep them both grounded. She had a wonderful sense of humor but put him in his place when he wasn't focusing on what he should."

She paused, her eyes shifting from Wil to Gramps, then she continued. "My family has been opening its doors to folks for as long as I can remember. I've met everyone from the poorest of the poor to royalty and everyone in between. And I'm speaking from my heart here when I tell you that your parents are probably the most special people God ever brought into our home. Their presence is still here. And it's in you."

Wil blinked away tears pooling in his lower lids as he tried swallowing past the golf-ball-sized lump in his throat. "Did they talk about me?"

"Oh my, yes. You were their pride and joy. As much as they loved their time here, they couldn't wait to get back to you. In fact, the last words I heard them say was how they'd have to bring you back here some day. And, well, it looks as though they did."

Anya pulled herself up, stepped over to Wil, and held his face between her palms. "Everything in life happens for a reason, my dear young boy. Good or bad. Your parents were living proof of that. And as rough around the edges as that one over there can be, he's trying to show you that. Listen. Watch. Take in what you learn the next little while. Take advantage of this time. Life changes in less than a second sometimes. Be ready." Then she gently patted Wil's cheeks and left the kitchen.

Wil chewed the inside of his lip. Gramps tapped the sides of his mug. They looked at each other and, for the first time since they'd started their journey, Wil was eager to go on... to see what else he had to see.

"Ready?" Gramps shoved his cup aside.

"Ready."

They walked through the grand sitting room to the front door, creaky boards moaning their farewell. They found their bags already there, with a bonus lying on Wil's bag. He drew in a sharp breath.

"I think they'd have wanted you to have that." Anya stood at the bottom of the stairs.

Wil picked up the framed picture of his parents that had been on the nightstand. He allowed tears to overflow and trickle down his cheeks. Without thinking about it, he walked up to Anya and hugged her tiny frame into his chest. He didn't remember his grandmother, but she felt close enough to that.

"Thank you. For everything."

"Oh, my goodness. You are more than welcome, love. You make sure you come back here one day. Even if I'm not the one to greet you at the door, you'll always have a room here."

"You'll be here. If you're anything like Gramps, I'm sure you'll be here for a long time to come."

Wil let Anya go then noticed the other two sharing a look. He couldn't place if it was filled with sadness or worry but before he had a chance to ask, Anya pointed at Gramps.

"Now you go easy on this young man or you'll have me to answer to, you got that you old coot?"

"Wonderful. Now I got two of you riding my back." Gramps gave her a half-smile and held his arms out to her. She walked up to him and they pulled each other into a deep embrace. "You take good care, Anya. Thanks for the good food, the chat and, as always, the good company."

She gave him one last strong squeeze then looked him right in his eyes. "You remember what I said to you. No regrets, no fear. Be at peace now. You've got this one to carry it on."

Gramps' eyes glistened. Then he nodded, bent down to grab his duffle bag, and opened the front door.

Wil stitched his eyebrows. "What was that all about?"

"You'll find out very soon."

Of course.

As the two men started down the sidewalk, Anya called from behind them. "Wait. One last thing." She had her camera in her hands, ready to take a shot. "Stand right there."

She snapped two pictures then put one hand on her chest. "There. Now I'll always remember this day. Safe travels, my dears. And see you again very soon, both of you. One way or another."

Gramps blew her a kiss then turned to walk to the truck. Normally Wil would have gotten sick of all the cryptic mumbo jumbo. He knew he was missing something, but for some reason it just didn't matter right then. His heart told him the next part of the trip would be the hardest. He looked down at the picture of his parents and was ready for it.

Wil tossed his bag in the back of the truck beside Gramps' then noticed two fishing poles and a small tackle box. He frowned then got into the truck.

"What's up with the fishing stuff?"

"Know a great fishing place your dad and I went to. Thought we could go on the way back. Interested?"

Wil started the engine, letting it warm up for a few seconds before saying, "Never been. Why not? But I'm not squishing worms on hooks."

"There are those girl panties again. Fine, ya wuss. I'll bait ya up."

"I am not a wuss or have girl panties. I simply don't like

shishkabobbing living things on hooks. Plus they're gross." Wil moved the car into drive then said, "So? Where to now, *monsieur*?"

"We need to go up to Park Meadows Drive in White City. There'll be a dirt road we'll have to turn off on to get to the last place. I'll let ya know where to go."

I don't doubt it for a second, Wil thought.

"We'll just fill up the gas tank on our way out of town, and we'll be off."

Next stop? Who knows. But Wil was ready for it.

Chapter Eleven

The ride from Indian Head to White City was supposed to take just under an hour. For the first twenty minutes, neither man said a word. Wil was grateful that they still got radio reception out there or the silence would have been smothering.

He flicked a look at Gramps, who hadn't changed his position since they'd left Anya's bed and breakfast: resting his chin on his fist, staring out the open window. He stayed that way even during the gas stop.

So much had happened in the last week. Gramps had revealed more about himself during their road trip than he had the entire time Wil had been living with him. Why *now*? Why was Gramps suddenly being so open about his life and his past? Why did Wil need to know all of these things at this point in his life?

Yeah, yeah. He got that he needed to learn how to be a man. But Wil's gut told him something deeper was going on. Something Gramps wasn't totally coming clean about. Or ever would.

Wil was about to ask Gramps for a bottled water when a

pop close to the sound of gunfire made him jump. Immediately after that, the car jerked to the right. Gramps threw one hand up on the ceiling and gripped the dashboard with the other. Wil struggled to keep the truck from rolling over by steering hard to the left and slowing down. He knew if he slammed on the brakes too hard they'd either skid or roll into the ditch — neither of which he had any desire to do.

As the truck slowed, and he had total control of it, Wil drove off to the shoulder and stopped. He turned the flashers on then started taking off his seatbelt. "You okay?"

Gramps nodded, releasing a slow breath. "Don't you worry about me. Been through worse. What the blazes was that?"

"I have a feeling one of the tires blew."

Wil undid his seatbelt then jumped out of his door. He walked around the front. Both tires were fine. As he got around the passenger's side, he saw the back tire completely flat and practically hanging off the rim. "Back right," he yelled to Gramps.

The old man opened his door and hung his head out to take a look. "Ah, dang. You remembered the spare, right?"

Wil tilted his head at him. "Of course."

"Crowbar?"

"Uh, yeah."

"Jack?"

"Gramps, I got everything in the back, including the tire iron. You saw me load it all up before we left. In fact, you reminded me three times to make sure it was all there before we packed up to leave."

"So? Why are you just sittin' there staring at it? It ain't gonna change itself. Let's get to it."

Wil shook his head and gave Gramps a half-smile. "Okay. Well, get out, then. I can't jack it up with you sitting in there."

Gramps got out and walked beside Wil, as he jumped up into the back of the truck. He handed down the crowbar and tire iron. The jack and crowbar were old-school and rusty. They would have been fine with his spanking-new tire iron that had both the screwdriver as well as the flat edge to pop the hub cap, but the old tools had been his dad's. They'd *had* to go with them.

Wil lifted the new tire to the side, and shoved it over. It landed with a thud right beside Gramps.

His grandfather screamed then jumped back, a cloud of dust slowly settling from the tire's impact. "Great green toads! You missed me by inches. Couldn't warn a guy you're throwing a tire at him?"

"Oh, for the love. You're standing there watching me, old man. If it had landed on you, it would have been your own fault. At least that's what I would have told the EMT people."

"Sleep with one eye open, you. That's not the first time you've almost given me a heart attack this week."

"Oh c'mon. Admit it. Would you have had nearly as much fun without me?"

"Maybe not but it would sure have been a lot quieter. And safer."

Wil jumped over the side of the truck and put his arm around Gramps' shoulders. "But you'll have so much more to tell your friends when we get back." He pulled the spare tire to its side and said, "Sam Hill knows I will."

Wil jacked the back of the truck up high enough to get the tire off then crouched to take the hubcap off. As he spun the iron around, removing the first of the four nuts on the tire, Wil decided it was as good a time as any to try getting a few questions answered.

"Gramps?"

"What?"

"What did Anya mean when she said, 'Be at peace now'?"

"How the blazes does changing a tire make you think of that?"

"Just answer the question, please."

Gramps clicked his tongue. "She was just reminding me that it's okay to let crap go. You know…"

"No, I don't. Why would she say something like that? Then she says she'll see both of us again one day, one way or another. Is there something wrong?"

"Stop reading so much into everything, boy. Sometimes a sentence is a sentence. Nothing else."

"But—"

"Nothing else. Now get movin' on that tire or I'll take over."

Wil took out the last nut, cursing under his breath at Gramps' stubbornness then pulled the tire off. He dragged the flat tire to the back of the truck and leaned it up.

After getting the new tire on, Wil lugged the flat tire up into the back of the truck, rolled the tools back up in the old towel he'd used to clean up, then joined his grandfather in the front seat for a drink of water.

"You did good, son." Gramps swigged the rest of the water in his bottle.

"Did you just compliment me?"

"Can't I just give you some praise without all the hubbub?"

"Maybe if it happened more often, it wouldn't be so shocking when it did."

Gramps flicked Wil a glare, ignoring his last statement. "That mechanic course was one of the best things you've done. Got some great skills and knowledge there to fall back on. That's something to be proud of."

Guilt pinched Wil's gut. The man was trying to be nice. "Thanks. It does feel good, actually."

"And I know your dad would be proud too. He's lookin' down on ya with a smile, seeing you work on this truck he built. Just… good for you is all."

"Thanks, Gramps. That means a lot to me. For real."

They sat in the cab with all the doors wide open, the

gentle, dry heat wind blowing through. Cricket songs flowed out from the wheat fields. One lone, cotton-ball-shaped cloud inched its way across the sky. Wil chugged down his water then got out to toss it in the recycling box in the back.

"Shall we get a move on, then?"

Gramps nodded, passing him three other empty bottles. "Yeah. We got ourselves a bit behind in schedule."

After tossing the rest of the bottles in the back, Wil went around and shut all the doors, stopping at Gramps'. "It's all good. Weird as it sounds, it was kind of a nice break… you know…?" He slammed the door, got in his side, and started the engine. "Should only be another twenty minutes or so, according to the GPS readings."

"I never thought I'd live to see the day when I'd actually understand what the Sam Haiti that means."

Wil laughed. He turned the flashers off, put the truck into drive then pulled back out onto the highway. "You know what I think?"

"What's that?"

"I think Dad blew the tire out to make us stop. Then he could join us, kinda. Ugh. I think we've been hanging out too much. That sounds nuts."

He felt Gramps' hand on his shoulder and glanced over at him. Tears flooded the old man's eyes behind his glasses. "I don't think that's nuts, son. I've felt him the whole trip." He put his hand back in his lap. "But you made a good point about spending too much time together. We'll definitely need some space when we get back home."

A smile tugged up Wil's lips. They passed the road sign signaling the turnoff for White City and the nervous butterflies that had made an appearance from time to time that week returned in Wil's gut. He had no idea why he was suddenly so nervous about their next stop with everything else that had happened to them up to that point. But whatever it was seemed to bring both sadness and worry to Gramps' normally stern face.

And it scared the crap out of Wil.

****

Gramps fired out his directions. "Go down here until we get to Park Meadows Drive. There'll be a dirt road on the right we need to turn down. I'll tell ya when to stop."

"Fine, fine. Man! It will sure be great driving without you as a front seat driver after we get home."

"Can you just drive without all the hullabaloo?"

At Gramps' signal, Wil turned onto a gravel road that beat the crap out of the bottom of the truck. Tiny rocks and sand pulled the wheels this way and that. Wil would never admit it to his grandfather, but he hated driving on gravel roads. They took the control right out of a person's hands. Driving in thunder or snowstorms were the only other things that scared him more.

Wil gripped the steering wheel so hard his knuckles turned white. He just hoped Gramps didn't see, or he'd tease him something awful.

"Shouldn't be too much further." Gramps squinted, trying to see through the dust. "There. Right there. Pull over to the side."

Wil saw nothing but a huge cloud of dust from driving up the road. He couldn't see if there were cars coming from the other direction or even where to pull over. He slowed right down to a crawl. As he did, the dust seemed to clear a bit, and he finally saw that there was a bit of a shoulder before a ditch on either side of the road. He parked the truck then looked over the hood to see the shadow of a building of some kind.

"C'mon." Gramps was already getting out. His voice softened. "Follow me."

As they walked through the dust cloud, Wil bet they looked like a couple of angels appearing out of the mist. They got closer to the structure and Wil was able to make out that it was an old house. A pretty big one, too, for the days it must have been built in.

A big porch extended out from the front door. Its double gates hung wide open, welcoming visitors into its warm and inviting breast. The floorboards were crooked and the railing was half gone, but Wil imagined the ghosts of the family who used to live there. An old lady rocking in her rocking chair, Mama snapping beans, kids chasing each other around the porch and down the stairs while Papa leaned on the railing and smoked his pipe — master of all he surveyed.

"Awesome." Wil whispered.

"Yep. Not as fancy anymore but still standing." Gramps nodded to it. "This was my first house."

Wil stared down at his grandfather. "You never told me that you lived out in the country. I thought you always lived in the city."

"Oh, for the love of sweet cakes, boy. Haven't you been listening to me all this time? I thought you woulda gathered that from all the places I've showed you and have told you I've been to."

"Uh, you never came right out and told me you were a country dude. You made it sound like these were places you just visited or whatever."

"Oy. I keep forgettin' that I have to just say stuff straight out to you or it flies right through your ears before stopping to register."

"Nice. What would also help is that you make sure I know you're actually talking to me so I'm not tuning out what I think is just you mumbling to yourself."

Gramps shot a glare up at Wil. "Enough! C'mon. Let's see what's still standing inside."

Wil's muscles tensed. Yes, he knew it was probably a crappy time to start throwing their usual banter in, but he was nervous with how Gramps acted. The old man never got mushy or sentimental unless something serious happened. Like when he'd had to tell Wil that his parents had died or when flecks of his dad appeared in his face as he grew up. Wil was much more comfortable with Gramps' dark sarcasm and yelling than when he was softer.

He shook his head to clear his thoughts and saw that his grandfather had already gone up the stairs. He jogged to catch up with Gramps and the two of them entered the front door. They stood in the middle of what looked like the living room. There was no glass in the windows. The dust from the road and the long-forgotten fields blew in, settling on everything left in there.

Wil suddenly felt overwhelmed with emotion. It was as if someone sat on his chest, making it hard for him to breathe properly. He instinctively put his hand over his heart in an attempt to slow it down as the house seemed to envelop him completely. It seemed like it tried taking him back almost a century... like it wanted him to see, hear, and experience the past.

The bottom floor was all one room, so Wil saw clear across to the kitchen with its manual pump for water and the wood-burning stove. The counter and cupboard space would make any modern woman jealous. There were dusty old jars of pickled stuff in a pantry on the left, with what he assumed to be an empty gun cabinet on the right. A stone fireplace just outside the kitchen looked like it used to have pipes going out from it to the upstairs for heat. A rickety old staircase — smack-dab in the middle of the room — led up to the second floor where, he guessed, the bedrooms would have been.

Gramps took a deep breath then said as he exhaled, "Ahh. I can still smell Gram's beef stew and biscuits. Don't cook like her anymore, son."

Wil frowned. "Wait a sec, I'm confused."

"Well, that's a shocker. What is it now?"

"Ha ha. No, seriously. You lived with your grandparents?

I thought they died when you were a kid."

"Granddad died long before I was born. Gram went to live with my parents after that, and the three of them came over here from Wales. I was born right here in this house."

Wil cringed at the thought. Not really about his grandfather being born there — that was kind of cool. It just dawned on him that back then there hadn't been the same medical facilities. People had had their kids at home, unmedicated and unassisted, and prayed for the best.

The sparkle in Gramps' eyes that Wil had noticed a few times on their trip whenever he reminisced about his past was back. Wil guessed his grandfather felt like he was still "with it" when he could remember stuff. He decided to keep that thought to himself right then.

Gramps tugged on Wil's arm. "Let's go upstairs."

Wil worried Gramps would have trouble with the stairs, especially after their visit to the church. But the old goat scaled them better than Wil did.

The upper floor was quite small by comparison. There were only two bedrooms up there, one at each end of a narrow hallway. The one on the left of the stairs was fairly small, while the one to the right took up the whole space on that side.

Gramps' voice echoed around the open space. "That there was my parents' room." He pointed to the small room then moved his hand to the right. "And this was where Gram, me, and my brother slept. Not much privacy, but ya took what you got back then and kept quiet about it."

"Whoa! A brother? You have siblings? Wow, Gramps. You never told me any of this. Not that it's surprising."

Gramps got quiet and dug his hands deep down in his pockets. "Yeah, well, there's lots you don't know about me, son. That's why we did this trip, why I've been showing you everything I have, and talking to the folks we met. And why I brought you here."

Wil's mouth was so dry his tongue stuck to the roof of his

mouth. His nervousness immediately turned into full-blown anxiety. He did not like where the conversation was headed.

Gramps held his stance, staring into his old bedroom. "Sure you'll hear lotsa crap once I'm six feet under."

"Shut up, Gramps." Wil nudged him with his elbow. "Besides, you're gonna outlive us *all* just to say you can." Wil laughed, but Gramps stayed quiet. "Okay, what's going on? For real this time. No more cloak and dagger bull."

"Dying ain't funny, son," Gramps said to the floor in front of him. "It's a part of life, and it'll come to us all. But you respect the dead, boy. They never leave you."

Wil's gut galloped, its acidic juices swirling around in his arid mouth. "What aren't you telling me?"

Gramps kept his eyes on the space in front of him for what felt like hours. Then he spoke in a tone that Wil hadn't heard since his parents had died.

"I had a brother, a twin. His name was George. We were close, but I don't remember him much anymore… his face has faded as time's gone on. He got a fever back when there was no medicine to fix stuff like that. Mama wouldn't let me go near him. Guess she was afraid I'd get it too. Here. Right here's where he died."

He paused, wringing his hands in his pockets.

"Go on. I'm listening." Wil patted his grandfather's back.

Gramps breathed in then continued. "We'd just buried him, then Gram died the next week. Must have been the shock of a young one going too early, I guess. Few months later, Dad went out to find work during the thirties when farmin' was scarce and other work even scarcer. He never came back. We got word there was a machine accident. No survivors."

"Oh, Gramps. I—" Wil started before Gramps jumped in again.

"Was just me and Mama then. Left me the man of the house. Had to take care of her. So we left this house behind and moved to the city. Mama didn't want to go. Guess she wanted to wait for Dad to come back, but we both knew in our hearts he wasn't gonna. Couldn't let her stay here waiting. So I got a job in a wool factory. Didn't pay much but it kept a roof over our heads, food in the fridge, and I learned all about the business. Mama died after only a few months in the city. Broken heart, I suppose. Too much loss for one heart to take. Then I was on my own. Just like you, son."

Wil let tears slide down his cheeks. *Why is he telling me all of this* now? He wiped his face on his sleeve.

As if reading Wil's thoughts, Gramps looked back at him with his piercing blue eyes. His jaw clenched so tightly the bones connecting it to his skull stuck out.

"See why you came to me, son? We're a lot the same, you and me — too much loss too early. Don't you go worrying, though. A rough start just makes you stronger. *I* made it. Started my own wool business from the ground up. Did it because I had to. I ain't gonna be here forever, boy. One day soon, it'll be just you. Oh, you'll have your uncles and aunties. But you ain't gonna have *parents.* Nobody to steer ya right when you go down the wrong way. You'll make it, though. I know you will. Here, I got something for ya."

Gramps pulled his hands out of his pockets. One hand grabbed Wil's hand while the other put something in it. The mysterious object was still warm from being in his pocket. When Gramps stepped back, Wil brought his palm closer to his face. The object was a military medal of some kind, shiny silver but very old, hanging from a red and blue stripped ribbon.

"My Dad's." Gramps' voice went hoarse. "Got it for bravery in the war. Gave it to me just before he left. Anytime I got scared about being the man of the house, I took it out. It's yours."

"Gramps, I can't—" Wil tried handing it back to him, but the old man clicked his tongue.

"Great balls of fire, boy! I'm trying to be sentimental here.

Just *take* the blasted thing!" He put his hands over Wil's again, his voice softening. "Please, boy. Just keep it with you like I always did, and you'll be just fine."

Wil felt tears rising again. "Why didn't you give this to Dad?"

"He didn't need it as much as you do."

Wil nodded and stuffed the medal deep in his pocket. Gramps nodded back then turned to the top of the stairs.

"Oh. And you better keep it all shined up or I'll come back and give ya a whoppin'." Gramps went back down the stairs.

Wil laughed, watching him stomp down the staircase. *You crazy old fart*, he thought, wiping his eyes. *You crazy, wonderful old fart.*

Gramps screamed from below, bringing Wil out of his thoughts. "Get a move on, boy. I need something to eat."

"Coming."

Down on the main floor, Wil stopped in the front doorway and turned around to soak in the house's atmosphere once more. He swore he heard the voices and laughter Gramps must have grown up with. Right in that moment, he didn't pay attention to the sadness or death. Only the happiness.

Wil walked out onto the porch and closed the door behind him. As he followed Gramps back to the truck, the anxiety that had ravaged his body a few minutes earlier eased. He still wasn't entirely convinced that Gramps had told him everything, but he felt closer to him than he had his entire life. And it was all good.

The two men got into the truck and clipped their seatbelts. Wil looked at the old house as he started up the truck. Like the other houses around there, it'd be gone soon too. On an impulse, he grabbed his cell from the compartment under his seat then held it out to the house.

"What in blazes are you doing?"

"I'm taking a picture of your house."

"That thing takes pictures too? Good gravy. One day they'll have one doodad that will cover everything."

"Getting pretty close, actually."

Gramps blew a raspberry. "Freaky space-type stuff. Nonsense…"

"Can you please just let me take this so we can go?"

"What's stopping you? Making sure the lighting is right? It's a house, son. In a field. Sitting in a flurry of dust. It ain't going to be a Picasso. Just snap it and let's go."

Wil ignored his grandfather, got the house in focus as best as he could then froze the moment. He wanted to bring the ghosts of the house home with them so they'd always have that slice of their life close by.

As they pulled back onto the dirt road, Wil said, "So? Shall we start back in the morning?"

"Sounds like a good idea. Won't be as long a ride on the way back. We got no stops to make."

"Actually, I think we should make one stop."

"Well, don't keep it to yourself."

"Let's go fishing at that lake you and Anya told me about. You know, where you and Dad went?"

Gramps kept his eyes straight ahead, but Wil saw a smile pulling up the side of his mouth. "I think that'd be a good lunch stop."

So do I, old man.

Chapter Twelve

For the first half-hour of the drive, the two argued over creating a solid plan of action. It was finally agreed upon that they would go to the truck stop that Gramps and Wil's dad had stayed at to eat and then stay overnight in the attached motel. The stop was a short twenty minutes from Mitchell Lake, their fishing destination.

Great, Wil thought. *Dining and sleeping with truckers. This should be the feather in the cap for this trip.*

"Don't you go makin' jokes about truckers and embarrass me," Gramps said. "Not all of them are how you see 'em in the movies. They work hard at what they do. It takes you away from family and friends for long stretches, but it's honest work and good pay."

"It creeps me out when you do that."

"What now?"

"Read my mind."

"Boy, I only thought you were losing your mind when we started this trip. Now I know it for sure. And for the record, even if I could read your mind I wouldn't. That's a scary place to go to visit, never mind owning it." He pretended to shiver.

"Ha, ha, hilarious. My mind is in stellar condition, I'll have you know. Or it was before this trip. If I'm losing it, it's your fault. At least that's what I'm telling the shrink while he's sizing me for a straightjacket."

"Mmm-hmm. Don't need one for your arms. You need one for that trap of yours. And I doubt they have one strong enough."

"Don't make me slam this truck into park and boot you out, old man. Wouldn't faze me one bit to leave you out here in the Saskatchewan boonies."

"Bah! I'd make my way home. You, on the other hand, would probably cling to your little girl panties and cry."

Wil stuck his hand up. "Okay, okay. Enough! Stop with the panties stuff, already. It hurts my feelings." He turned his head from his driving for a second and fluttered his eyelashes. From the corner of his eye, he saw Gramps giving him a deadpan stare.

"Uh huh. And you wonder why I question your need for the panties."

"Watch it. Now how much further do we have to go to get to this fine dining and sleeping establishment?"

"Well, since we've been driving for about three hours now, I'd say we're almost there."

They made small talk, as nicely as they could, for another twenty minutes, then Gramps said, "There it is there. Over on the right."

It was exactly what one would picture such a place to look like. A small, two-level motel was at one end. Wil counted sixteen doors. In the middle was a greasy-looking diner and at the other end was some kind of bar that Wil was scared to look at, never mind go inside of. Up closer to the highway were four gas pumps and a small convenience store. There were six semis lined up at the Trucks Only parking area.

Well, if this doesn't scream 'date night,' I don't know what does, Wil thought.

Gramps pointed to the motel. "Let's get a room first, then we'll grab some grub."

"Perfect. But you aren't making me go in that bar, got it Mr. Party Animal? I don't feel like getting my arms ripped off trying to defend your feistiness."

"Panties."

Wil parked the truck in front of the motel office then stuck his tongue out at Gramps. "Can we please just get this over with?"

The two men got out of the truck and grabbed their bags from the back. The place was full, but they were in luck that one guy was just checking out when they arrived.

"You'll just have to wait about an hour or so while we clean the room up for you," the motel clerk said. She reminded Wil of Kathy Bates from that movie where her character had kidnapped her favorite author and ensured his stay by breaking his ankles. He repressed a shudder.

"Sounds good," Gramps said. "We'll just go grab some dinner and come back for the keys."

Dinner. Yes, Wil thought, staring at the diner appetizingly called The Grease Pit. *I wonder what delectable culinary delights we'll have to choose from there.*

Gramps swatted Wil on the shoulder. "Well, it ain't no five-star fancy restaurant, but at least you know you're getting home-cooked food here."

"I see one fly in my food or a big, hairy, sweaty dude in the back doing the cooking and I'm outta there. I'd rather eat vending machine crap than put my system through that."

"This from a boy who ate fries with gravy and cheese the other night as a bedtime snack. Shut it and let's just go."

The mention of the fries sent hungry pings through Wil's stomach. He realized he hadn't eaten anything since Anya's breakfast of champions. *Oh well. Maybe they have good soup. Can't mess that up too much.*

Wil opened the door for Gramps then followed him

through. Surprisingly, the place had a real homey feel. With the red faux-leather booths, red-and-white-checkered tiling on the floor, and the long table and stools in the middle of the place, it had the feel of a true '50s-style diner. Old rock-and-roll music flowed out from the jukebox in the back, and the place was spotless. Wil was impressed.

"There are two stools up at the counter," Gramps said. "Let's sit there."

Wil scanned the backs of all the truckers also sitting at the counter. "Uh, aren't there any booths open?"

"Oh, for crying out loud! No one's gonna bite ya, boy. People are here to eat. No one cares about you. If it makes you feel better, I can hold your little hand."

"Funny. You know those stools are pretty high up. You might need a boost. Or I can get the waitress to find you a ladder."

"Don't you worry about me. You just get on over there and plant your butt."

They walked down to the end of the counter and hoisted themselves up on to the last two stools. When Gramps sat down, his stool spun, nearly throwing him to the floor. Wil grabbed it with one hand and threw the other out to catch his grandfather.

"Holy Hannah. What is it with you and chairs lately? First one tries to devour you, then you almost get shot across the room by another."

"I don't even get respect from inanimate objects these days."

"'Inanimate, huh? You been reading 'Word of the Day' in the paper again?"

"Oh, knock it off. I know a fancy word or two. Just don't feel the need to use 'em all the time."

"Well, you've just used one for today. Better pace yourself and save the other for tomorrow."

Before Gramps had the chance to give his usual snarky

response, the waitress came down to their end and slapped her palms on the countertop.

"Well, look at this. I don't believe I've ever seen you guys here before. And I'd remember that sweet face." She touched Wil's cheek. "So, what'll you be having, boys?"

"I'll start with a coffee, madam." Gramps pulled two menus out from the condiment holder and handed one to Wil.

"You got it, handsome. What about you, young pup?"

The woman had to be in her late forties or early fifties. She reminded Wil of his Aunt Mae, only more tired. "Uh, I'll just have water, please."

"Polite too, huh? Boy. Nice to see some young ones with manners nowadays. Good job, handsome." She winked at Gramps. "Take a look at the menu. Special today is roast beef platter with cherry pie. Soup is cream of potato. Be right back with your drinks."

She sauntered back down the line, grabbing empty plates and flirting as she went. The tension in Wil's body eased.

"See? Told ya it wasn't so bad. Your dad loved this place. I think that's the same waitress we had back then."

"Why am I not surprised?"

"What's that supposed to mean?"

"You know everyone."

"No I don't. Just that things don't change as quickly out here as they do back in the city. And people stick to what they do for a living a lot longer. Change is good, but consistency is better."

"First of all, Confucius. Second? You just used up your second fancy word."

"If we weren't in public, I'd slap you upside the head."

"It's never stopped you before."

The clanking thud of something striking the top of the counter made Wil jump. The waitress had brought them their drinks while they'd been scrapping.

"Boys, boys. There's no fightin' allowed in here. Do I hafta use my wrestling moves on you to get you to behave?"

"Sorry, madam. My grandson here sometimes lets his mouth run off without making a pit stop at the brain."

"And my grandfather forgets to take his happy pills."

The waitress folded her arms on the counter, leaned down, and let out a belly laugh. "You boys are quite cute, I hafta say. Nice to have that around here. And although I appreciate the gentleman-like 'madam' reference, I'd rather y'all call me by my name while you're here. Alice."

Gramps smacked the countertop. "Hot blazes, I *knew* it was you! I was in here a while back with my son. Name's Wilf Carter, and my boy Craig was about his age at the time. He spilled an entire glass of pop on ya…"

Alice stood up, tilted her head, and squinted at Gramps. "Oh my stars, yes. I remember you. We get all kinds coming through here but most everyone is regular. I never forget the new ones that drop in. Yeah. I'd just started here. Your son made me a little flustered. Quite a looker he was." She shifted her gaze to Wil. "Wow. You're the spitting image of him, cutey."

Heat radiated in Wil's cheeks. "Um, thanks."

"I thought you lived in Winnipeg. What the heck are you doing out this way?"

"Road trip," Gramps said. "Takin' this boy on the same one my son and I had done back then. We're just on our way back. Gonna do some fishing over at Mitchell before heading the rest of the way."

"How nice. Lake was stocked last week, so you should catch a couple at least. Well let's get you on your way, then. What'll it be?"

Wil was hungry but didn't want to overeat so close to bedtime. "I'll have the soup and a corned beef on rye."

"Got it. What about you, darlin'?"

Gramps scanned the small menu one last time then said, "I'll have the roast beef special. Extra gravy, please."

"Alrighty. Coming right up."

Alice shoved the paper with their order on the wheel for the cook and shuffled away to do coffee refills. While Gramps poured way too much sugar and cream into his coffee, Wil scanned the place. As he noted in the other places they'd stopped, the people were so different in the small towns. They seemed happier... more relaxed. There wasn't one person in there sporting a three-piece suit or talking on a cell phone, texting or typing away on a laptop. Everyone was actually talking to each other.

Some of the guys at the counter joked with a group of people sitting in the booth behind them. Alice walked around chatting with every customer and introducing people to others. It was like a big, huge family. Normally Wil couldn't stand the idea of strangers talking to him. He was one of those guys who walked with his head down, not making eye contact. Not because he was a snob or too busy, but more because he didn't want the hassle. He started realizing that making that time probably wasn't such a bad thing.

Gramps snapped him out of his daydream. "Oh for Jiminy Cricket's sake. Am I gonna be talking to myself through the entire meal again? Didn't you hear a word I just said?"

"No, I was tuning you out. What? I'm listening."

"I was just saying that maybe we could go shoot a game of pool before heading back to the room."

Wil stitched his eyebrows. "Are you insane? Oh wait. We established that a few miles back."

"What the hay? One game of pool. Scared to get your butt whipped by an elderly, decrepit man?"

"You are so not decrepit and you know it. *That's* the problem."

"I'll be good. How much trouble can we get into?"

"I don't think you really want me to answer that after everything that's happened, do you?"

"C'mon, boy. One game. Used to be quite a shark in my

day."

Wil rolled his eyes. "Of course you were."

"No, really."

"Uh huh. I'm kinda good myself, you know. Me and my buddies go every week, remember?"

"Sure. But you guys probably have no clue what you're doin'."

"Tell you what, you old geezer. You are on. One game."

"One game."

"And you aren't allowed to stir things up, mister. You start a bar fight, I'm not bailing you out."

"Would expect nothing less."

They held a look, each with a smirk on his face, then Alice brought their meals over, placing their plates in front of them.

"You boys need anything else for now?"

"No thank you, Alice. I think we're good," Wil said.

They ate their meals in silence. As Gramps put the last piece of pie in his mouth, Alice came over with the bill.

"How was everything, boys? Notice your plates are pretty clean there."

Gramps scraped bits of crumbs and cherry smears with his fork. "Have to say, this is one of the best meals I've had in a while."

"Nice to hear. Well, if there's nothing else, I'll give you this."

Both men reached for it at the same time.

"Well, I'll let you sort it all out. Come back again soon, you hear? Don't be strangers." She sauntered over and hugged a refrigerator-sized trucker that had just sat down.

"Tell you what," Wil said, his hand still on the bill. "You pay for the meal, and I'll pay for the round of pool. I may as well since I'm going to wipe the floor with you."

"Deal. And don't be so sure about that, son. Looks are deceiving."

"Do tell."

Gramps left money to cover their dinner, plus a very generous tip, then he and Wil went to the bar next door, simply called Frank's. The place was dimly lit and had a country-western feel. The bar was positioned in the middle of the place right up against the right wall. Booths lined the left wall all the way to the back where the pool tables were. In the middle were a few tables and chairs.

"Want something to drink?" Gramps cricked his neck towards the bar.

"You know I don't drink. Especially not because of what happened to Mom and Dad."

Gramps put his hand on Wil's shoulder. "I know, son. Me neither. I meant water or a pop."

"Oh. Yeah. No thanks. I'm still too full."

"All right, then. Let's go over and pay for a table."

"Let's get it on."

There were only a few other patrons in Frank's. Wil guessed it picked up as it got later. He wondered if Gramps had brought his dad there. He remembered his dad had been quite good at pool too.

"Okay. Let's go," Gramps said. He shuffled past Wil through the tables to the back of the bar. Wil followed him, then grabbed two pool cues from the wall.

"Be prepared to lose, old man."

"Oh, we'll see smart-butt. Rack 'em up and let's do this."

Wil got the balls ready while Gramps chalked up his cue.

If someone had told me a few weeks ago that I'd be playing pool with my grandfather, I'd have arranged to have that person's head examined.

They flipped a coin to see who'd go first, and Gramps won the toss. He positioned the white ball, leaned over, and lined up his shot. He pulled the cue back, but when he went to hit the ball he accidentally let go of it, sending it across the table.

"Oh, for the love… must be a little rusty."

Wil sputtered out a laugh. "A little rusty? Good grief. Don't embarrass yourself, Gramps. Really. Let's just go back to the room."

"Just take your turn and shut up. I said we're gonna play pool and that's what we're doin'."

"Alrighty. Whatever you say Mr. I-Can't-Even-Hold-On-To-My-Pool-Cue."

"Make the break Mr. Going-To-Have-A-Sore-Butt."

Wil released a throaty laugh then leaned over to make the break. The room echoed with the crack of the white ball crashing into the triangle of balls in the center. He didn't get any balls in right away but took his first shot.

"Number eight in the corner pocket," he said. He made the shot, and the ball rolled into the pocket. He smirked at Gramps, who pouted on the other side of the table.

"Number ten in the side." That time he made the shot, but the ball hit the rim and rolled back. "Well, do your best. Would you like me to strap your cue on your arm for you this time? We wouldn't want you to impale someone."

"You know what? Why don't we make this interesting?"

"What did you have in mind?"

"How much you got on you?"

Wil opened his wallet. "I got forty bucks on me."

"I'll bet you that forty bucks that I can clear this table."

"Okay, now I *know* you've lost it. You do that, old man, and not only will I pay you this money, I'll bait our hooks when we go fishing."

"And you gotta clean the bathrooms at home for a week."

Wil cringed. "Deal. And if I win, you gotta pay me forty bucks and… hmm… you can't give any rude or sarcastic remarks for a week, including to Mr. Clark next door."

"You're asking a lot there, son. That man is as loopy as a roller coaster at the fair."

"Thought you said you weren't worried about losing."

"I'm not."

"Then put your money where your mouth is."

"You asked for it."

With that, Gramps picked up his cue, shuffled around to Wil's side of the table, leaned over then set up his shot. "Ten in the side." Gramps slid his pool cue back and gave the ball a sharp tap. The ball shot across the table and slammed into the hole.

Wil let his jaw fall slack.

Gramps shifted sideways. "Four in the left corner." Gramps wound back and shot again, sending the white ball crashing into the number four ball, which hit the seven in front of it. Both balls dove into the corner pocket. "Close your mouth, boy. You're gonna start drooling."

Gramps went around making every shot like a pro, even ones Wil had never seen guys his own age do, never mind one Gramps' age. After only a few minutes, Gramps cleared the table, leaned his cue against the table, and stuffed Wil's money in his front shirt pocket.

"Don't try to con a con, my friend. You'll lose every time. And didn't I tell you to close your mouth? It's just getting embarrassing now."

"Where… How…?" Wil stammered.

"Back in the Second World War, me and a buddy of mine spent a lot of time at the local bar playing pool. Got quite good. So good, we played in a lot of the competitions out there. Won most of them. The best was when we got to snaffle know-it-all boys out of their money."

"Oh good. Not only have I found out my grandfather has a connection to the mob, saved two lives *and* was some sort of secret agent op guy in the war, but now I find out you were a pool con too. I have never been more proud."

Gramps shrugged and raised up his hand. "Told you there were lots you didn't know about me. Got lotsa layers. Like an onion."

"I was going to say snake, but okay. All right, you. I'm broke now, so let's get going. And if you tell my friends about this, I'm going to put you in an old folks' home."

"Lips are sealed."

"I don't think even strongest glue on the planet could accomplish that feat."

"Don't push it, Panty Man. I can forget I promised not to blab to your friends. I'm an old man, doncha know. Memory is fadin'."

"Yeah, yeah. C'mon."

Gramps grunted at Wil then shuffled toward the door.

Shaking his head, Wil watched his grandfather walk away from him for a moment. That man had more surprises in him than a clown at a kid's birthday party. If he was going to have his rear whipped at pool, it couldn't have been by a better person.

He turned back to look at the table, smiled then caught up to his grandfather in the doorway.

When they stepped outside, Wil grabbed Gramps' arm, making him turn around. "You are an amazing person, Gramps Wilf."

"And you're well on your way."

Gramps gripped Wil's hand, gave it a squeeze, then said, "Right. Let's hit it for an early night. Fishing's best early."

Wil actually felt sad that the trip was close to an end. But he had one more question he had to ask Gramps. And the man was going to give Wil the answers he needed whether he liked it or not.

Chapter Thirteen

Wil was woken up by a pillow whopping him over the head.

"Wakey, wakey," Gramps said. "The fish ain't going to wait forever."

"How many times do I have to tell you not to wake me up like this? Can't you just play music or talk sweet and nice? Why must you hit and yell?"

"You should know by now that sweet and nice isn't my style. Besides, if I was all gentle with getting you up, you'd still be here next Tuesday, snoring away."

"Well at least I'd be well-rested. What time is it? And if it's any earlier than six, I'm going to have to hurt you."

"Five-thirty."

"For the love..." Wil grabbed the pillow, still over his face, and threw it back at his grandfather. "No person in his right mind should ever be up at this hour."

"Guess you should get up, then."

"Don't push it, you. I haven't had coffee yet."

Gramps tossed the pillow back on his bed. "Made a pot. Get up, shower, have a cup then let's go. Wanna be heading out by six."

"What about breakfast?"

"We'll grab some muffins and fruit from the store when we stop for bait."

"Well, look at you, Man With the Plan. All right. I'm up."

Wil sat up and swung his legs around. He felt like he'd been run over by a semi. He hoped the last stretch of their trip would be less… exciting than the first part had been.

"And by the way?"

"What's that?"

"I'm really lookin' forward to watching you get all girlie baiting our hooks. Wish we had a camera." Gramps laughed.

"Well by all means. Please use the camera on my phone. Goodness knows we'll need to share it with the world. Perhaps you'd like to film it and submit it to the television station? The entire city should be able to share my pain. Hey! I can even wear my panties for ya. That'll make it a feature."

That made Gramps laugh even harder. Wil tried his best to hold his composure but seeing his grandfather doubled over with laughter, something he rarely did, was too much. Both men let go until they had tears rolling down their cheeks.

After a few minutes, Gramps put his hand over his chest. "Dang it. Haven't laughed like that in years. Coulda killed myself."

"Well, dying of laughter is better than dying from opera."

"No crap. Okay. Enough stalling. Let's get goin'."

Wil got up, poured a cup of coffee then headed off to the shower. Even though the thought of spearing worms grossed him out more than he was willing to admit to Gramps, he looked forward to the fishing experience.

Maybe Dad will be there too.

****

After a twenty-minute car ride and a pit stop at the store

for worms and breakfast, Gramps and Wil walked up the path to Gramps' special fishing spot. Mitchell Lake was a fair-sized, open lake. Their special fishing spot was a massive log lying across a huge bolder sticking out from the shallow part of the water. It was surrounded by tall pine trees and was pretty secluded.

Gramps led the way up to the middle of the log then sat down, allowing his legs to dangle just above the water's surface. Wil followed him, putting the bait on one side of him and their coffees and muffins between them. It took Wil longer than normal to bait the hooks, losing a few worms in the lake from jumping at their slimy squirminess. But soon enough, they were all baited up, casting their hooks into the water, drinking their coffee.

The calm water ebbed up to the log. A fish jumped in the distance, teasing the two fishermen. A loon called from somewhere along the shoreline. Frog song creaked from behind them. Wil's body completely relaxed. It had been quite a while since he'd felt so at ease and worry-free.

Now is as good a time as any...

"Gramps?"

"What?"

"Can I ask you something?"

"Ya just did."

"You know what I mean."

"Boy, if you have something you wanna talk about, spit it out already. You know I hate all the dramatics."

Wil swallowed hard. "Tell me about the accident. I want to know what happened."

"I was wondering how long it would take before you finally asked. Noticed your thoughts taking you away quite a bit this trip. I harassed you, but I knew. Been thinking about them a lot too."

"Yeah..."

"Well, what did you want to know? Where should I

start?"

"I don't know. Anywhere."

"I wasn't there, of course, so I don't know exactly what happened. Know that they hit a semi head-on. The truck driver was drunk and driving in the wrong lane. With the rain storm they were driving in, I'm guessing the road conditions were bad enough to affect reaction time."

Gramps paused, giving his line a light tug then continued. "From what the police report said, your parents' car smashed right into the grill of the truck. Your mom wasn't wearing her seatbelt. She went through the windshield. She didn't suffer. Died instantly. You don't need to know any more than that. Your dad must have hit his head on the window or something because he had brain trauma. Plus they hit the truck so hard, the front of the car was pretty much crushed. Even though the airbag deployed, your dad's body was whipped forward, snapping his spine like a twig." He shook his head and rubbed his chin with his palm. "The pictures were horrible..."

Wil's eyes were warm with tears. "Pictures? Why were there pictures of such an awful thing?"

"They gotta for the reports and stuff. And if the family wanted to press charges."

"Did we?"

"What?"

"Press charges?"

"In the end we decided not to. The trucker died of his injuries, and your dad was in a coma for weeks. There had been enough crappiness. We let it go."

"If I had been older, I would have. Someone should pay for taking the lives of others, especially doing a dumb-butt thing like driving drunk."

Gramps put his hand on Wil's knee. "The man died, son. His family was left behind having to not only deal with what happened to *him* but also what he caused. He left kids behind too. He paid for it. Enough punishment, right?"

Wil shrugged. "How many kids did the guy have?"

"Five. All under ten."

"The man had five young kids and drove loaded? I just don't understand that."

"I know, son. Some folks just don't think. We all make mistakes—"

"That's so much more than a mistake, Gramps. That dude *chose* to drink, and he *chose* to get in his truck after. That's not a mistake, that's intentional."

"All right, all right, now. Enough. Can't hold onto all this anger, son. As hard as it is, you gotta let it go. Even if it's bits and pieces at a time."

Wil took a few deep breaths to calm his pounding heart. "I know. I'm trying." He rubbed his palm on his thigh. "Tell me about after... about Dad. And what they did with Mom."

"Well, like I said, your dad was in that coma for weeks. Once they determined he had no brain activity, the doctors suggested to pull the plug. Hardest decision I ever made."

"You decided?"

"Yep."

"Were you the one who pulled the plug too?"

"Yep. Had to."

"Why?"

"No one else could do it. Plus I was his daddy. Me and your gran gave him life. If his life had to be taken, one of us had to do it. And since your gran wasn't with us anymore, I had to be the one to send your dad on."

The two men didn't speak for several minutes. Wil wiped his cheeks with the back of his hand then looked over at Gramps, who was doing the same thing.

"Where are they buried?"

"In Winnipeg. Was going to take them out to be with your gran, but we wanted to keep them close. Why?"

"I want to see them. Can we go there before we go right

home?"

"Sure, but... are you sure you're ready for that?"

Wil paused. *Am I? Am I ready to say goodbye? To accept that they're gone? To... let it go?*

"Yes. I think I finally am."

Gramps nodded his head once then said, "Okay, then. We'll take a detour when we get to the city. Proud of you, son. Takes guts."

"I think you've taught me all about that this last week."

Suddenly Gramps' rod bent down. "Hot cross buns! I think I got a bite!"

He struggled to get up but almost slipped, so Wil shot up and grabbed his rod. "Wow! Feels like a big one," Wil said. "I'll bring it in for you and then we can take a pic—"

Just as Wil started reeling it in, he lost his footing and fell head first into the water. Fortunately, the water was shallow enough for him to stand waist-deep, so he kept reeling. Gramps' chesty laugh echoed around the small bay.

"Holy Hannah, boy! That's the funniest thing I've seen in a while."

"I'm glad you're amused. Can you keep it down back there? It's hard enough to do this way."

"Oh good grief. We don't need the fish that bad. Let 'er go and get back up here."

"What? After the booger pulled me in? Forget it. It's coming home with us."

Wil reeled and pulled until he got the fish right beside him and pulled it up out of the water. It dangled from the hook, flopping its tail in his face. "Got it!"

"Say cheese, son." Gramps captured the moment on Wil's cell phone camera.

"Wonderful. Thanks for that, really."

"Don't worry. I got your good side. If I knew how to work this thing, I'd fire it over to that news feller."

"Your empathy and support are overwhelming. Now, do

you think you could take this stinky, slimy thing so I can get out of here?"

Gramps took the rod, removed the fish from the hook then whacked it on the log.

"What the heck did you have to do *that* for?"

"Gotta put it out of its misery. Suffocation is not a pretty way to go."

Wil waded over to the log, climbed up, and took his runners off. "Neither is having your head plunked against a hard surface." He dumped the water out of his shoes and Gramps was in stitches again.

"Holy catfish. I haven't laughed this much in years."

"Again? Thanks for laughing at my pain. Let's get going. I need to change into some dry clothes. Do we have something to wrap that thing up in for the ride home? We obviously can't leave it here now that you've maimed it. Haven't you ever heard of 'catch and release'?"

"Yeah. But I think we were past that when you let it flop around all over the place too long. I think we got a few freezer bags in the back. Then we'll take the water out of the cooler and put it in there. Should be fine for the rest of the trip."

Wil took his socks off, then they gathered up all of their stuff and headed back across the log toward the path. He walked on tiptoes behind Gramps, the forest floor scraping up the balls of his feet. When they got to the end of the path and Wil was finally able to walk flat-footed on the cement, Gramps grabbed his arm.

"Listen, 'cause I'm only gonna say this once. This trip meant a lot to me. Really did. And out of everything we did, this here was my favorite part. One day you'll understand all that's been goin' on here… and what I've been sayin'. And, hopefully, you'll know why I've been so hard on you. It never was because I didn't think you could be great. It was more because *I* knew you could and *you* didn't."

Wil held back firing out a sarcastic reply and simply

gripped his grandfather's hand. He had the entire ride home to harass him anyway.

"Thanks. For real."

"Sure. Now. Let's get you changed. Wouldn't want ya to get all chaffed, what with your sensitive skin and all."

"Nice. Wanna put some baby powder on my butt?"

"Don't even go there. Just shut up and get goin'."

Gramps walked toward the truck, and Wil turned back, gazing at the path behind them.

I'll take this with me always, he thought. *Hope you got it all, Dad and Mom.*

****

Mitchell Lake was the middle point in the trip back to Winnipeg so the duo decided — actually, Gramps decided — that driving straight through would be the best idea. For some reason, Gramps wanted to get back to the city as soon as possible. Normally Wil would have been suspicious why the old man was suddenly so eager to end their trip when he'd been making them stop every few hours on the way out. But, honestly, he was ready to go back home.

They drove ten hours back to Winnipeg, stopping only for food, bathroom breaks, and once for gas. Their conversation was surprisingly light, with very little banter. Gramps seemed exhausted near the end of the trip, nodding off in the middle of a conversation about some of the pranks he and his army buddies had played on their superior officers.

For the last hour, Wil had allowed his thoughts to take him back to the last time he'd seen his parents. It had been when his parents had taken him to his grandfather's house before their last vacation together... ever. During the recent trip with Gramps, he'd pieced together that his parents had planned on going to Anya's Bed and Breakfast. He remembered the conversation in the car among the three of them. As always, his mother had worried whether everything had been going according to plan, while his father had been more laidback about things.

"Did you remember to grab Wil's blanket and his favorite stuffy?" his mother had asked. "I left them both on top of his suitcase."

"Check on the blankie, and Rufus is back there with the boy," Dad had responded. "Hold up your bear to back me up, Wil."

Wil had held Rufus up as high as his arms could stretch so his father could see it in the rearview mirror.

"See? All taken care of."

"What about his routine schedule?" Mom had put her fingers on her chin. "Did you pack that in his suitcase? I mean, your dad means well, but he doesn't always... you know... seem to hear what I tell him."

"Yeah I saw that. Honestly, he isn't gonna read it. You know that, right?"

His mother had squinted her eyes at his dad, but didn't respond. "His vitamins?"

"Yup."

"His rain jacket and boots?"

"Yep."

"Sunscreen and sunhat?"

"Oh for the love of all that's good in the world, woman. He's got a change of outfit and gear for every possible weather turnout. And if there's a combination of weather, like say, sunny with a chance of rain, he can put things together to be completely covered. It's only for a week. He'll be fine. Gramps will be fine. We'll be back soon enough, right Wil?"

Wil had nodded his head, not realizing at the time what the future held for them all.

The most significant thing that stuck with him from the last moments with his parents was the love they'd all had for one another. Just before they'd left on their trip, his parents had both squatted down to his eye level and they had a group hug.

Then his mother had said, "Goodbye, my sweet Wil. You be a good boy for your grandfather and mind what he says. Remember that we love you and are with you even when we aren't right here holding you."

"Yeah. And don't let that old guy push you around. You gotta push back once in a while, or he'll get used to being in charge," his dad had said.

Wil had turned his head to look up at his grandfather standing right behind him. He had smirked back down at him.

"Bah. Just shut up and get a move on." Gramps had waved his hand at them. "He's been here before for a lot longer and we've done just fine. Haven't we, boy?"

Wil had nodded, then Gramps had put one hand on each of his shoulders and pulled him into his torso. Wil had squeezed Rufus to his chest as tightly as he could, trying to be a brave boy and not cry.

"We'll be back in just over a week with tons of stories to tell. Goodbye for now," Mom had said. They'd waved, blown kisses, and they were gone.

Gone.

Wil's entire body prickled with goose bumps as he was brought out of his thoughts by Gramps' hand on his forearm.

"You okay, son? You looked a million miles away."

"Not that far away. Maybe about thirteen years or so." Wil eyed the sign welcoming travelers to the city of Winnipeg, then he flicked Gramps a look. "So? Where is it?"

"You sure you're ready? It's fine if you want to settle in first. No rush."

"No. I want to do it. I… need to."

Gramps gave Wil's arm a light squeeze. "All right, then. We gotta make one stop first."

****

Wil's parents were buried in a cemetery on the south side of Winnipeg in the St. Vital area. After another half-hour, the two men stopped at a flower shop a block from the cemetery then slowly made their way to their final destination of the road trip.

"We can take the truck through the place, since they have a road winding around it. It's pretty big. Just stop at the front office there so we can check in."

"I didn't realize we had to do that."

"What's that?"

"Check in to a… cemetery. Just seems weird."

"Don't have to, I guess. Just a courtesy. Come in with me, son."

"Oh, Gramps. Do I have to? I mean, come *on.* Isn't this hard enough?"

"You want to do this, you do it right. Your mama would have wanted you to meet the folks that have been taking care of her and your daddy all these years. Now c'mon. Just leave the engine on."

"What if someone steals the truck while we're in there?"

Gramps looked over the top of his glasses at Wil. "And just who is gonna do that in this place, son?"

Wil raised an eyebrow. "Fine."

They got out of the truck then entered the wide-open front door of the office. They were greeted by a couple that looked about as old as his parents would have been. The tug of familiarity he felt when he looked into the woman's eyes was so overwhelming he had to put his hand on Gramps' shoulder so as not to fall over.

"Saints alive, Vern! Look who's here." The woman walked out from behind the counter, her arms stretched out to them, and embraced Gramps. "It is wonderful to see you, Mr. Carter."

"Oh for heaven's sake, Claudia." Gramps patted her back. "I've told you over and over, 'Mr. Carter' is way too formal for all we've gone through. 'Sides. We're all too old for such stuff. Just call me Wilf."

Claudia giggled. "Fine, then. Wilf." She stepped back, her hands still on Gramps' biceps, and looked at Wil. "I can't believe my eyes. Is this Becca's sweet little Wil?"

"One and the same. Wil? This is Claudia. She was your mama's best friend and your godmother."

Wil was glad to be leaning a bit on Gramps or his wobbly legs would have given out on him. "Godmother?"

"Yes. I was there when you were baptized. Guess I haven't been doing a very good job being your spiritual guide. I checked in with your grandfather here frequently, but he made it clear that you were quite adamant about not going to church. Religion isn't something that should be forced on you. I thought I'd wait until you came to me. And you still can."

A month earlier, Wil might have stormed out of the place with the offer. Right then, it didn't bother him at all. In fact, it was something he thought might be... okay. "Thanks. I'll keep that in mind."

"So, I'm guessing you are here to see your parents," the guy Claudia called Vern said, still behind the counter. "They've been waiting a while to see you."

Wil shifted his eyes to the floor and chewed the inside of his cheek. "Yeah... well... I..."

Fingers touched his chin and gently guided his face up. "You don't owe anyone an explanation. We all grieve in our own way, and God gives you the tools you need to deal with your pain as you are able to handle it."

Claudia went back to the counter and grabbed a pen and paper. She wrote something down then handed the paper to Wil. "This is our phone number here. Whenever you need a chat, or anything, you call. Anytime."

Wil took the paper, folded it, then put it in his back pocket. "Thank you. I will."

"Well, let's get goin' then," Gramps said. "Don't wanna

keep them waiting."

"Do you need me to draw you a map, Wilf, or are you okay?" Vern walked around to join his wife on the other side of the counter.

"I think we're good, thanks, Vern. I remember where we're going."

Claudia gave each of them another hug, Vern shook their hands, and they were on their way. They got back in the truck then inched their way around the gravel road to near the back of the cemetery. As they came around to an area with plots lined up around an enormous oak tree, Gramps said, "This is it, son. Put 'er in park, grab your flowers, and let's go."

Wil's heart pounded so hard he felt his pulse in his fingertips. All the moisture in his mouth drained.

"You can do this, son. I'm with you."

Wil nodded then punched Gramps lightly in the shoulder. "Let's do this. But I'm relying on your sense of direction. Don't get us lost in a cemetery or I'll never speak to you again."

"Is that supposed to be a threat? You just watch out for empty graves. If you fall six feet under, I ain't saving ya."

"I think it's you who should be careful. You're closer to being down there than I am."

"Don't be so sure about that, son."

After some nervous laughter, Wil got out of the truck. Before following his grandfather down the path he grabbed a plastic bag from the back then scooted to catch up.

The place had to be ten times the size of the place where his grandmother was buried, and much older. There was a large section of white crosses in memory of lost or missing soldiers right across from them. Wil darted his eyes from that section to the back of his grandfather's head then shuddered.

I wonder how many of those men and women Gramps served with, he thought. *Or saw die.*

He shook his head to clear his thoughts. Gramps stopped

at a granite grave marker a few feet ahead of him. Wil's heart picked up an even faster pace and he walked slower. A couple more steps and he'd be facing the source of his lifelong pain. Was he really ready? Did he really want to make his parents' deaths... real?

He stopped in his tracks. Gramps turned his head then peered at Wil over his glasses. "C'mon, boy. You aren't doin' this on your own. I'll be right here. It's gotta be today. It's meant to happen right now."

Wil still couldn't move. It was as though his shoes had suddenly turned into cinderblocks, holding him back.

"You've gotten this far. You can do this. Please, son..."

Wil filled his lungs until they pressed against his ribcage, then he slowly released the air through his mouth.

I can do this.

He took a step, his knee quivering in response to his nervousness.

I have to do this.

Another step closer, the other leg shaking even worse.

Gramps didn't say anything, but held his hand out. Wil gripped it, looked into the old man's eyes, and nodded. Wil shifted his gaze to the headstone beside them. He still couldn't bring himself to look down. Once he did, everything would change. *He* would change.

Forever.

"Go on, boy," Gramps whispered. "They're waiting for you to say something."

Wil closed his eyes and swallowed hard. Gramps gave Wil's hand a gentle squish, then Wil felt his arm being tugged down. When he opened his eyes, Gramps was kneeling on the ground, still holding Wil's hand. And that was when he finally saw it.

The headstone was carved out of dark gray granite. His dad's nameplate was on the left, his mother's on the right, both carved directly into the stone. Their last name was etched into a shiny black stone in capital letters and pinned across the top of the marker: CARTER. Wil's knees buckled and he dropped down beside his grandfather.

He lifted his other hand and fingered the beautifully-crafted lettering, first the last name, then each of their separate nameplates. There they were. Gone.

Forever.

A wave of emotion boiled up in Wil. It rose higher and faster, like champagne bubbling up after the cork had been released. Then he screamed. He didn't have time to stop it and didn't want to. He yelled until he had no air left to make the sound, then he let go of Gramps' hand and collapsed forward.

Every emotion he'd held back from surfacing his entire life came spewing out with such force he thought his body would explode. As he cried, he felt small circular rubs up and down the length of his back — just like Gramps had done the first few months after Wil had moved in with him. In that moment, he no longer wanted answers to all of the, 'Why?' questions he'd had. He didn't want revenge on the man who'd made the fateful decision to drink and drive that night so many years earlier, killing his parents. He no longer felt angry or scared or bitter. He just felt... relief.

After what seemed like hours, Wil breathed heavily, as though he'd just finished the most intense workout ever. He slowly lifted up his body to a kneeling position. His eyes stung, his cheeks burned from the salty wetness covering them, and his throat hurt.

Gramps patted Wil's back once more, then stuffed a handkerchief in his hand. "That was the most honest dang thing I've seen you do in years, boy. Good for you."

Wil wiped his face with the hanky then blew his nose. "Please tell me this was a clean one."

"I admit nothin'."

Wil sputtered a weak laugh then looked up at the headstone. "Hi, Mom and Dad. Sorry about that. I guess I... I wasn't totally ready for what it would feel like to..."

He stopped, shifted his legs to cross-legged, and looked at Gramps. He gave Wil a sharp nod. Wil let out a shivered sigh then went on.

"I feel pretty crappy for not coming to see you sooner. I guess I just felt that once I did, I had to accept that you guys were gone. It hurt too much to do that. But, I guess, not accepting it is worse because... well... then it's like I'm kind of forgetting about you."

Gramps laid the bunch of white lilies across Wil's lap then gripped his shoulder.

"Here, Mom. I remembered these were your favorites. Gramps still has those bulbs we planted out in the back. They come up every year, just like you said they would." He gingerly arranged the bouquet under her name. "Dad? I have something for you too. I guess if you've been watching me like Gramps says you do, you know that I took that automotive course. Well, here's a copy of my certificate." He laid the paper under his dad's name then put a keychain with a small wrench dangling from it on top of it so it wouldn't blow away.

"Hey. I remember that thing," Gramps said. "He gave that to you one Christmas, didn't he?"

"Yeah. I think I was three or something? I don't remember a lot of stuff from back then, but I remember him giving it to me and saying one day maybe he'd teach me to use a real one."

"Well, look at that, Craig. He took the hint. Will wonders never cease?"

Wil shot his grandfather a side-glance then went on. "Anyways. I have one more thing that I brought for you." He reached into the plastic bag he'd gotten from the back of the truck and pulled out a framed picture. It was a picture of Wil smushed between his parents, each of them with beaming smiles, him frowning.

Gramps sucked in his breath. "Holy Hannah! Is that the picture I took of you before they left?"

"One and the same. You got it developed and framed it. You told me it was a way to keep them close until they got back."

"Well, shoot. That is wonderful, son. But you only kept it out for the first few weeks until..."

"Until I moved in. I know. I'm sorry. It just hurt too much to look at it, you know? I kept it in the storage bin in my closet." He held the photo closer to his eyes. "If I'd known this would have been the last time I'd have seen them, I would have smiled... or hugged them. I refused to even let Mom kiss me."

His chest tightened with the memory. He'd been angry with them for leaving him behind and, as all kids tend to do, tried punishing them through holding back affection. Looking back, that seemed so selfish.

"You were a five-year-old boy ticked off for getting shoved onto your grandpa so your parents could be alone. They understood. Don't beat yourself up anymore."

"I know that now. I think that was something I always held in too. I felt guilty for reacting that way." He placed the picture between their names and in front of the flowers. Then he said, "I never forgot about you. Ever. I don't want you to think that. I've learned a lot about myself and our family the last couple of weeks, thanks to this old dude. The most important thing I learned is that when you love someone, they never truly leave you. I am who I am because of both of you, and because Gramps made sure to keep me afloat, even when I tried hard to drown myself."

He ran his fingers over their names one last time. "Mom? Thank you for the hugs and kisses I can still feel. And for your pearls of wisdom I often catch myself using. Dad? Thank you for your sense of humor and your car skills. I will treat the truck better than the most valuable thing on earth. Most of all, thank you for your love, even from wherever you are. Without it, I wouldn't be here."

Then he kissed his fingertips, pressed them into their last name, and stood. Gramps grabbed Wil's forearm, using it to pull himself up. They stood side-by-side staring down at the headstone then Wil put his arm around his grandfather.

"Let's go."

As they walked back down the path to the road, Wil looked over his shoulder and whispered, "I'll be back soon, I promise. I love you."

They walked down the path in silence, arm-in-arm. As they got to the road and let go of each other, Wil noticed his grandfather's cheeks glistening with dampness.

"Why, you sentimental old fart. Are you crying?"

Gramps cleared his throat, digging another hanky from his pocket. "No. I'm sweating through my eyes."

Wil laughed a belly laugh, something he hadn't done much until recently. And it felt pretty good.

As they drove out of the cemetery, Wil winced when Gramps honked his nose into the handkerchief. "You seem to have an endless supply of those things."

"A gentlemen always has one handy just in case."

"I truly hope to the stars above that you are cleaning those on a regular basis."

"Some things are best left a secret. Now shut up and drive. I gotta pee."

Wil smiled and shook his head.

I hope this is the last step in our grand adventure, he thought. *No more doors need to be closed anytime soon.*

At least I hope not.

Chapter Fourteen

The week after Gramps and Wil's adventure, Gramps died of a heart attack right on the eighteenth green during his annual Golf For MADD game. Word had it he had signs all throughout his golf game, but he was winning and wouldn't go to the hospital. Stubborn old fool — a pain in the rump right to the end.

Gramps hadn't wanted a huge funeral or a big fuss made over him. The family had a wake with close friends, including Anya, Reverend McInnis, and little Dakota. The funeral where they'd lay Gramps to rest would just be family.

Wil sat in Gramps' recliner in the den while the rest of the family chatted with people. He had no desire to be social. He flipped the footrest up and leaned back. The chair still smelled like Gramps' cheap drugstore cologne. He closed his eyes, trying to clear his head. He heard the murmur of chatter from the living room. Someone laughed. There was clanking of dishes from the small spread his aunts had prepared for their guests. Suddenly, a familiar small voice broke through the other noise.

"Hi, Wil."

He opened his eyes to see Dakota peeking around the sliding door. He pulled the back of the chair up straight and waved her in.

"Get in here, you."

She slipped in, walked up to him, and gave him a hug. "I'm so sad to hear about Gramps. I liked him, even if he was super grouchy sometimes."

"I'm sad too, kiddo. But he wouldn't want us to be, right? Those are the things that made him grouchy. He'd want us to remember him and talk about him, though."

"Okay. We can do that."

Dakota sat on the footrest and the two talked about everything that had happened to them. "If it hadn't been for you guys, I wouldn't be with my mom now."

"Hey. How is your mom? Did you come with her?"

"No. She's in chemo again and not feeling very good. I came with my grandma. She's talking to one of your aunts. They know each other really good, I think."

Wil remembered the conversation with Gramps about Dakota's family. "Yeah, they do. That's cool. Why don't you get out there and have some food? My aunts make some awesome cake and cookies."

"I saw. Okay. I'll come back later to say goodbye. Are you gonna come out there?"

"In a bit. I just want to be alone right now."

"Oh, okay. I totally understand. I feel that way too sometimes. See you later."

"See ya, girl."

She gave Wil one more hug then left. He rested his head back again and, not even a minute later, he heard the door slide open.

Why is it when you want to be alone, that's when everyone thinks you need company?

"Look, I appreciate everyone checking in on me, but I really just want to be alone right now, okay?"

"Well, that's fine. I'll just sit here with you. I need some alone time myself."

He recognized the voice right away and opened his eyes. "Oh, Anya. It's so awesome that you could come up. Gramps would love to know you're here."

She winked. "Oh, he knows I'm here, love."

"Yeah. You're probably right."

"There's something I need to tell you. I don't think he'd mind my sharing this with you."

"Okay."

"I actually knew you guys were coming up. He called me a couple of weeks before, telling me all about it. I thought it was a brilliant idea, considering all he was dealing with at the time."

Wil snapped the footrest back down and leaned forward. "Dealing with what? Was he in some kind of trouble?"

"Oh land sake's no. It was nothing like that. Your Gramps had been having trouble with his blood pressure and heart for months before you came out my way. He was on medication and was being monitored closer than usual. The doctors started growing more concerned about him because the medication wasn't working anymore. They told him it was only a matter of time before his old, beautiful heart gave out."

Wil shook his head. "He never said a word about that."

"And he wouldn't have. You know him. Loved him to bits but, goodness, what a stubborn old coot he was."

That's the biggest understatement of the year, Wil thought. He hadn't even known about all the medication Gramps was on, not that he was surprised. The man had kept most of his life a deep, dark secret. Why the heck would he discuss something as minor as his bad health?

Suddenly, their adventure made total sense: Gramps' sudden need to go on the road trip, why he'd given Wil his dad's truck, the reasons behind every stop they'd made and every person they'd met along the way. He just wished his grandfather had been more upfront about everything. Maybe he wouldn't have been so hard on the old goat. Or acted like such a selfish doofus. All the man had wanted was to show Wil the side of his life he didn't trust with anyone else. And Wil hadn't appreciated it at the time. His throat tightened.

Anya stood up, steadied herself on the armrest of the recliner, then leaned down and gave Wil's cheek a light kiss. "Anyway, I should be going back to my hotel, dear boy. It was a long, tiring trip out here, and an even more emotionally draining day. I'm going to go enjoy my memories of your granddad and have a nice rest. I'll see you tomorrow at the funeral. I'm one of the few asked to come."

"He would have — I mean, he will — like seeing you there."

Anya patted Wil's shoulder. "You have to know you meant the world to him, my boy. He adored you. You brought light into his life. And I am so glad that you had each other for as long as you did."

With that she left him alone, sliding the door closed behind her. There didn't sound like there were as many voices in the living room, so Wil decided he'd make an appearance. He sat for a few more minutes then went out.

Everyone seemed to have left except his aunts, uncles and their spouses. He stopped by the dining room table to grab a mini meat sandwich when his Aunt Dorothy called him.

"Wil, honey. Can you come in here for a second? We need to talk to you about something."

Wil sighed deeply then shoved the rest of the sandwich in his mouth. *Man. There's a reason they call them 'finger sandwiches.' That's about the size of them.* He figured a person needed to eat at least four to equal a normal-sized sandwich. He picked up an egg salad one then walked into the living room. He sat next to his aunt on the couch and almost choked on his sandwich.

There on the mantle was a framed picture of him and

Gramps — the one Anya had taken when they'd visited her. A wave flooded over him from his knees to the top of his head. He was so glad he was sitting because he was sure he would have crumbled to the floor. Then he allowed himself to cry, almost as hard as he had when visiting his parents.

It was a release that had been building up since the night he'd found out his parents had died. Sure, he'd unpacked a huge load of emotional baggage at his parents' gravesite, but he hadn't allowed himself to let it all out. Back then with Gramps, he'd mourned the loss of his parents. And with Gramps' strength, he'd finally been able to face that demon. But in that moment, seeing the picture of him and Gramps, it dawned on him that he was alone.

Well, not completely alone, of course. He had his aunts, uncles, cousins, and friends. But for the first time in his entire life, he truly had no parents. No one to guide him or love him the way a caregiver loves a child. No one to lean on, get advice from, or give him a hard time if he steered off his path. No one to share the good stuff with or to help him get through the crappy stuff. And it hurt. But he knew that Gramps would have wanted him to let it out, even if he got his rear teased off in the process.

All of his aunts surrounded him, offering their comfort. Wil was closest to his Aunt Dorothy. She pulled him into her side, wrapping both of her arms around his body, and let him bawl. He cried until his eyes hurt and the heavy feeling in his chest disappeared. Then he sat up, wiped his face with the tissue his uncle handed him, and flopped back.

"I'm sorry. I... I don't know what came over me. I guess the picture got to me."

"Well, for heaven's sake, Wil. It's completely understandable. We all loved Gramps, but you had a very special relationship with him. And with all that you've been through, I'm glad you let it all out. Are you okay?"

"I will be. What was it that you wanted to talk to me

about?"

Dorothy shifted her position to look right at him. "Well, you know that we read the will yesterday, right?"

"I know."

"It wasn't very long. You know Gramps. Blunt and right to the point…"

He gave a weak smile.

"We'll talk about the other stuff in there later. You know… not the right time for money talk. But one thing he did ask was that you do the eulogy at the funeral. He said there was no better person to do the job. Are you ready for that?"

Wil shook his head and looked up at the ceiling. *You had this planned all along, didn't you, you old fart?* "Yeah. I'm up for it. I'll bet we all have a few stories to tell about that crazy old man."

Everyone shared their favorite Gramps memories. Laughter filled the house.

It was nice to have laughter again.

****

The family stayed with Wil in Gramps' house. It was already up on the market for sale and the family thought it wouldn't stay long. The price was right, the neighborhood was highly desirable, and the market was good. Wil hated seeing the For Sale sign on the front lawn, but, well, life must go on.

Wil tried for the fifth time to knot the tie on his monkey suit. After slowly letting go of it, thinking he'd finally conquered it, the tie fell open again. He growled, ripped the tie off his neck then threw it on the floor.

"Stupid piece of crap!" he sputtered through gritted teeth. "If we have to wear these torture devices with buttons, the very least they could do is give us lessons on how to put the flippin' tie on."

Wil heard a knock on the door, then Aunt Mae popped

her head in. "You okay, Wil? Need some help?"

"No, thanks. Everything set?"

His aunt dabbed her nose with a tissue and sniffed. "Yep. Whenever you're ready."

"Be right down."

After Aunt Mae left, Wil's thoughts drifted. He missed that old goat. He missed the crack-of-dawn wake-up calls. He missed his heart-racing, army-strength coffee. He missed their banter and his wonderful sarcasm. The only thing he didn't miss was having the heat on. He blinked to clear away the tears that threatened to flow. Gramps wouldn't tolerate any more crying anyway.

The tie mocked him from the floor.

Forget it. I'm not trying again.

Looking at his naked neck in the mirror, Wil knew Gramps would threaten a whoppin' if he went out like that. He actually heard his squawk: *"Great green toads, boy! You aren't going out there dressed like that. You'll embarrass me. If I have to wear a stupid tie, you know you are too."*

Wil snickered then stuck his hands deep in his pockets, wringing his hands around for an answer.

Suddenly, a smile spread across his lips.

****

As Wil and five of his cousins lifted Gramps' casket up onto their shoulders, Gramps' medal beamed in all its glory from Wil's neck. He'd just shined it up that morning.

Gramps would be proud.

Don't get cocky, son. Just shut up and drive.

About the Author

Chynna Laird is a freelance writer and award-winning author. Her passion is helping children and families living with Sensory Processing Disorder and other special needs. She's authored a children's book, two memoirs, a young adult novella, a young adult paranormal/suspense novel, a contemporary new adult novel and an adult Suspense/Thriller.

She is always looking out for the next challenge to conquer. She loves reading, writing, The Beatles and letting her sillies out with her four children. Her favorite expression, and one she lives by, is, "Telling me I can't do something only makes me work harder to prove you wrong."

Made in the USA
Charleston, SC
25 October 2013